STORIES TO SHARE WITH MY PARTNER BOOK 10

Camden Books Publishing

José F. Nodar

Stories to Share with My Partner Book 10 / José F. Nodar
ISBN: 978-1-7643409-6-0 - Paperback
ISBN: 978-1-7643409-7-7 - E-Book
ISBN: 978-1-7643409-8-4 - Audiobook

Dedication

In loving memory of my wife,
Miriam Vassallo Nodar,
and her enduring presence.
You are always in my thoughts.
For anyone who's ever loved deeply, lost fully, and still found
the courage to begin again

TABLE OF CONTENTS

FOR THE SAKE OF A DREAM

We sat on her tiny balcony, two mugs of coffee cooling between us. Sunlight poured over the railing as if it were trying to eavesdrop. The street below bustled with noise, but up here, everything felt suspended, like time knew this conversation needed space to breathe.

"I think I have to crush her dream," I said.

Claire stopped mid-sip, blinking at me over the rim of her mug. "Wow. That's not where I thought this chat was going."

I sighed and dropped my head into my hands. "I know how that sounds. Horrible. Evil-stepmother level stuff. But hear me out."

Claire set her mug down slowly. "I'm listening. Carefully. And judging you only a little until I understand."

I gave her a weak smile. "It's Amelia."

Her lips parted. "Oh."

"Yeah. She messaged me last night, ecstatic. Said she finally found an agent. After everything… the rejections, the exhaustion, the nights she almost gave up. I was so happy for her, I actually cried. Like, cried."

Claire was nodding slowly. "That's incredible, right? Isn't that what she wanted?"

"It should be. It would be. Except the agent is fake." I picked at the edge of my mug, not looking up. "Like super fake. Fiverr-profile-selling-book-promo fake."

She froze. "No."

"Yes."

Claire drew in a breath as if she were preparing for a wave. "And she doesn't know?"

"Worse. She tagged them on her bio. She's proud. Happy. Hopeful. She's finally feeling like herself again. I've never seen her post like that; full of joy, like she's back in her skin."

Claire leaned back, her expression softening. "So, you're stuck between letting her believe in something that's a lie or telling her the truth and maybe breaking her heart."

"Exactly." I rubbed my forehead. "And I don't even know how to start the conversation. If I say it wrong, if I come across as even a fraction bitter or jealous, she'll never believe me. She might think I'm trying to sabotage her."

Claire studied me, head tilted. "Do you think she'd think that of you?"

I paused. "Not usually. But you know how fragile things have been for her lately. She said last month she was considering quitting writing altogether. And now this feels like the universe finally throwing her a bone. Like her pain wasn't for nothing."

Claire nodded slowly. "But if she signs something, gives away her rights, pays money…"

"She'll be crushed either way," I finished for her. "Later, when she finds out. Maybe publicly. Maybe after she's written this agent into every hope and plan for the next year of her life."

We sat with that for a moment.

"You love her," Claire whispered. "You just want to protect her."

I nodded, throat tightening. "She's better than me, Claire. Genuinely. I've read her manuscripts. She's got this raw, honest way of writing that leaves you wrecked. She should be on shelves. She deserves a real shot."

"So," Claire said, wrapping her arms around her knees, "do you really have to crush her dream? Or do you just need to nudge her gently toward the truth?"

I blinked. "What does that mean?"

"I mean… maybe you don't go in there with torches and pitchforks screaming 'IT'S A SCAM'," she said, mimicking an old-school town crier. "Maybe you approach her as her friend. The same one who's always believed in her. The same one who offered to help her publish herself."

I tilted my head, considering. "You think if I just, what, ask questions?"

She nodded. "Yeah. Like: 'Hey, I was curious about your agent. What's their background?' Or 'I noticed they also do book promo. Did you vet their client list?' Let her connect the dots. Offer to help check stuff. Make it collaborative, not confrontational."

"Like we're solving a mystery together, not me coming in as judge and jury."

"Exactly," she said. "You plant a seed. And when she's ready, she might start to question things herself."

"What if she doesn't? What if she doubles down, defends them, and accuses me of being unsupportive?"

Claire reached out and touched my hand. "Then you've done what you could. You approached with love. With care. That's all you can do. She's still her own person. You can't make her see something she's not ready to."

I looked down at my lap, her words settling into the folds of my thoughts.

"But if you say nothing," she added gently, "and something worse happens, you'll hate yourself more."

I laughed, short and dry. "I already kind of hate myself."

"Hey." She squeezed my hand. "You are not the villain here. You're the reluctant protagonist in a complicated plot. You care. That matters."

I laughed again, this time with a little more breath in it. "God. You always know how to make things sound like fiction."

"Comes with the job description," she grinned. "Two authors on a balcony, solving ethical crises with metaphor and caffeine."

We sat there in silence for a beat.

Then I asked, "Do you think I should write it? Like, instead of talking? A message where I can say things clearly and carefully?"

Claire chewed her lip. "That might be wise. Gives her space to react. Time to sit with it before responding. Just keep the tone gentle. Encourage her. Remind her of her talent."

I nodded slowly, ideas starting to form. "Something like: 'Hey, I looked into your agent because I was so excited for you, and I noticed a few red flags. I don't want to upset you, but I'd hate for you to be taken advantage of.' That kind of thing?"

Claire smiled. "Perfect. Honest. Kind. Non accusatory."

"And I'll end with something like… 'No matter what happens, I'm still here. And I still believe in your work.'"

"Exactly," she said. "And mean it. Which I know you do."

"I do," I whispered. "More than she knows."

Claire leaned back and closed her eyes, letting the sun wash over her. "You know, this isn't crushing her dream."

I looked at her. "It's not?"

"No. It's helping her protect it. Dreams are fragile. Sometimes the kindest thing is to help someone see the cracks before everything falls apart."

"Damn," I said, sipping my now-cold coffee. "That sounded wise. Are you quoting a novel?"

She smirked. "Nope. That one was all me."

"Maybe you should be the one publishing this story."

"Only if you let me write it from the perspective of your anxiety-ridden inner monologue."

I laughed. "Deal."

The city kept moving beneath us, indifferent to the heartbreaks and hard truths whispered above it. But I felt lighter. Still scared, sure. But not alone.

And maybe that was the whole point of friendships like ours: to catch each other when the world got too heavy. To face the hard stuff together.

Even when it meant risking everything.

For the sake of a dream.

BUY NOW

"**D**ad," I sighed, dramatically flopping onto the vintage floral sofa; a relic from my grandmother's 'everything must match the wallpaper' phase. "I'm losing my mind. My boss just sent an email at 10 PM demanding 'synergistic results by EOD tomorrow.' My new dating app wants me to 'swipe right on destiny NOW!' And I just accidentally bought a subscription to 'Extreme Alpaca Grooming Monthly' because the 'confirm' button was strategically placed next to the 'no thanks' button—which was invisible."

Arthur "Art" Finch, my father—a man whose fashion sense peaked in the early 90s and whose wisdom often arrived via circuitous, anecdotal routes—merely hummed. He was meticulously polishing a miniature porcelain owl he had purchased at the op shop in the CBD of Northport NSW where we lived; a task he'd been engaged in for the better part of an hour.

"It's like the entire world is screaming 'DECIDE! NOW! QUICK!'" I continued, gesturing wildly. "Every app wants my decision in seconds. Every employer wants results this quarter. Every investment platform profits when I trade like a caffeinated monkey on a sugar rush!" I paused, catching my breath. "And my crypto portfolio? Let's just say it's currently performing a graceful swan dive into the Mariana Trench."

Art finally set down the owl, his eyes twinkling. "Ah, the siren song of the immediate. A dangerous melody, my dear.

An expensive one, too." He leaned forward, adopting his 'sage of the sofa' posture. "You know, your Uncle Barry once tried a get rich quick scheme involving artisanal, gluten-free kale chips. He invested his life savings, bought a dehydrator the size of a compact car, and convinced half the neighbourhood to pre-order. He was convinced he'd be a kale-chip baron by Tuesday."

I braced myself.

This was how my dad's lessons began.

"He worked himself into a frenzy," Art continued, warming to his narrative. "Sleepless nights, muttering about 'optimal crispness' and 'the kale-to-chip ratio.' He was convinced if he didn't launch now, someone else would corner the market on kale-chip-based financial freedom. Meanwhile, old Mr. Henderson, who lived down the street— you know, the one who always wore the same beige cardigan and spent his afternoons meticulously pruning his rose bushes?"

I nodded. "The one who smells faintly of mothballs and success?"

"Precisely!" Art beamed. "Mr Henderson, bless his heart, had simply bought a few index funds decades ago. He touched nothing. He traded nothing. He just existed. And last year, when Uncle Barry was still trying to offload 500 pounds of slightly too-chewy kale chips at a garage sale, Mr. Henderson bought that charming little cottage on Elm Street. Cash. He practically owns half the neighbourhood, that man. And all he did was wait."

I blinked. "So, the moral is what? Don't invest in kale chips?"

"Well, that's certainly a secondary moral," Art chuckled. "But the primary one, my dear, is this: impatience is an expensive emotion. It's the emotional equivalent of paying surge pricing for everything. Every time you feel that frantic urge to click 'buy now,' or 'invest here,' or 'swipe right on destiny,' pause. Take a breath. Ask yourself: 'Is this the kale chip dehydrator, or is this Mr Henderson's beige cardigan?'"

He picked up the porcelain owl again, stroking its tiny head.

"The world, Maya, is designed to make you impatient. It wants your quick decisions, your impulsive trades, your immediate gratification. Because that's where the profit is for them. But while everyone else is frantically chasing the next shiny object, the boring investor, the patient person, the one who just lets things simmer, they inherit everything the impatient leave behind. All the good deals, all the stable growth, all the peace of mind. They get the neighbourhood, the prime real estate, and probably a very comfortable retirement, all because they resisted the urge to panic-sell their imaginary kale chip empire."

I actually smiled. "So, I should be more like Mr Henderson?"

"Not necessarily the mothball smell," Art conceded, "but certainly the financial strategy. And the rose bushes. There's a lot to be said for a well-pruned rose bush, you know. It teaches patience."

He winked. "Now, about that 'Extreme Alpaca Grooming Monthly' subscription, perhaps you can negotiate a bulk discount for the entire neighbourhood? You never know when a well-groomed alpaca might come in handy. Just don't expect immediate returns."

I laughed, a genuine, unburdened sound. "Thanks, Dad. I think I finally get it. Less frantic swiping, more beige cardigans."

"Precisely," Art said, returning to his owl, a picture of serene, boring patience. "Precisely."

MISTAKEN IDENTITY

The insistent rapping on the door of Unit 3B at the Meadowbrook unit block in Surry Hills, New South Wales, jolted Frank Billingsly awake. Sunlight—a pale and unwelcome intruder—was just beginning to seep through the gap in the floral curtains. He groaned, burying his head further under the pillow adorned with embroidered kittens.

"Bill," he mumbled into the fabric, "someone's at the door."

Silence.

Frank sighed.

William B. Elworth, his roommate of fifteen years and a man whose morning routine involved a complicated series of stretches, herbal tea consumption, and the meticulous arrangement of his collection of antique thimbles, was likely deep in his pre-dawn rituals.

The rapping came again, louder this time, accompanied by a booming voice that could curdle milk. "Police! Open up!"

Frank's eyes snapped open.

Police?

Here?

At their humble abode, a sanctuary of mismatched furniture, half-finished jigsaw puzzles, and the lingering scent of lavender potpourri? This had to be a mistake. They were hardly hardened criminals. Their most rebellious act in recent memory was probably that time Bill accidentally walked out of the supermarket with a reusable shopping bag he hadn't paid for.

He'd returned it the next day, profusely apologetic.

He nudged Bill, who was now sitting upright in bed, eyes wide with alarm. "Bill! Did you... did you forget to return that library book about the history of cheese mites?" Frank whispered, his voice laced with genuine concern. Bill was meticulous about library books. Fines were anathema to him.

Bill, however, looked utterly bewildered. "Cheese mites? Frank, I haven't read about cheese mites since, well, never! What's going on?"

The banging intensified.

"Police! We have a warrant for the arrest of Frank Billingsly and William B. Elworth!"

Frank scrambled out of bed, pulling on his paisley dressing gown. Bill, equally flustered, donned his velvet smoking jacket—an item he usually reserved for evenings spent listening to classical music and pondering the existential angst of garden gnomes.

They shuffled to the door, a mismatched pair of bewildered retirees. Frank peered through the peephole. Two uniformed officers stood in the hallway, looking rather stern and slightly out of place amidst the pastel painted walls and the gentle hum of the building's ventilation system.

Frank fumbled with the locks and finally pulled the door open.

The two officers, a tall woman with a no-nonsense expression and a younger man who looked like he was still waiting for his coffee to kick in, stood before them.

"Frank Billingsly and William B. Elworth?" the woman asked, her voice firm.

"Speaking," Bill replied, puffing out his chest a little despite the tremor in his voice.

"You are under arrest for the theft of numerous library books," the younger officer stated, holding up a rather official looking document.

Frank and Bill stared at them, dumbfounded. "Stolen library books?" Frank sputtered. "There must be some mistake!"

"We have a warrant," the woman said, her gaze unwavering. "Please step outside."

Their neighbours, Ms Higgins from across the hall and young Timmy Henderson from down the way, who was on his way to school, had now gathered in the hallway, their faces a mixture of shock and morbid curiosity.

"But we love the library!" Bill protested, his voice cracking slightly. "We're regular patrons! I always return my books on time. Well, almost always. There was that one time with 'The Joy of Crocheting'…"

"Sir, please," the younger officer said gently, placing a hand on Bill's arm.

Frank, meanwhile, was trying to process this bizarre turn of events.

Stolen library books?

He enjoyed a good mystery novel, but he certainly didn't live one. The most clandestine thing he'd done recently was sneak an extra biscuit from the communal tea tin at the Tuesday afternoon bridge club.

"Could you perhaps tell us which books we allegedly stole?" Frank asked, trying to maintain a semblance of calm.

The woman consulted her notepad.

"The list is extensive, Mr. Billingsly. It includes multiple copies of 'Knitting for Beginners,' 'Advanced Sudoku Puzzles,' 'The Culinary Delights of Pickled Onions,' and 'How to Train Your Budgerigar to Speak Mandarin.'"

Frank and Bill exchanged incredulous glances.

"Budgerigars?" Bill exclaimed. "I can barely get my philodendron to thrive, let alone teach a bird a foreign language!"

"And 'Pickled Onions'?" Frank added. "I detest pickled onions! The mere thought is, well, repulsive." He shuddered dramatically.

Despite their vehement denials, the officers insisted they had to follow procedure. Handcuffs were produced, shiny and cold. Frank felt a wave of surrealism wash over him as his wrists were gently secured. Bill looked like he might faint.

"Don't worry, Bill," Frank said, trying to sound reassuring, though his own stomach was doing somersaults. "We'll get this sorted out. It's obviously a clerical error."

As they were being escorted down the hallway, Ms Higgins gasped dramatically. "I always knew there was something shifty about those two and their quiet ways!"

Timmy Henderson, wide-eyed, whispered, "Wow! Real handcuffs!"

The walk to the police car felt like an eternity. Frank kept expecting someone to jump out and yell "April Fools!" but the grim faces of the officers suggested this was no prank.

At the station, they were led to a small, sterile interrogation room. A detective with a weary expression sat behind a metal desk piled high with files.

"Frank Billingsly and William B. Elworth," the detective said, his voice flat. "We have a considerable amount of evidence linking you to the theft of numerous books from the Surry Hills public library over the past six months."

"Evidence?" Bill squeaked. "What evidence?"

The detective produced a blurry security camera still. "This image reveals two individuals matching your description leaving the library late at night on multiple occasions, carrying large bags."

Frank squinted at the picture.

The figures were indeed vaguely their height and build, but the image was so grainy they could have been anyone. And large bags? They usually left the library with a single tote bag containing their latest literary acquisitions.

"That could be anyone!" Frank protested. "We always return our books through the designated slot during opening hours."

"And these," the detective continued, laying out a series of library cards on the desk. "These belong to you, and they have an unusually high number of overdue and missing books associated with them."

Bill paled. "But those must be books we borrowed! We never stole anything!"

The detective sighed. "Gentlemen, the sheer volume of missing books, coupled with the security footage…"

Just then, the door to the interrogation room swung open, and a young, flustered librarian rushed in, clutching a thick ledger.

"Detective Miller!" she exclaimed, her voice breathless. "I think we've found the culprits!"

Detective Miller looked up, a flicker of hope in his tired eyes. "You have?"

"Yes!" the librarian said, pointing frantically at her ledger. "It wasn't Mr. Billingsly and Mr. Elworth at all! It was the Surry Hills Bookworms Brigade!"

Frank and Bill exchanged bewildered glances. "The Bookworms Brigade?" Frank asked.

"Yes! It's a group of local children who meet in the library after hours," the librarian explained, her cheeks flushed with embarrassment. "They've been 'borrowing' books for their secret clubhouse and haven't been returning them. We only just discovered their hideout in the old storage room behind the children's section."

A collective sigh of relief filled the interrogation room. Detective Miller looked slightly sheepish. "Well, gentlemen," he said, unlocking their handcuffs. "It seems there's been a rather significant misunderstanding."

Frank rubbed his wrists, feeling a mixture of relief and indignation. "A misunderstanding that involved handcuffs and a rather terrifying trip in the back of a police car!"

Bill, ever the gracious one, simply said, "So, we're free to go?"

The librarian apologised profusely, offering them a lifetime exemption from late fees and a complimentary bookmark. Detective Miller even managed a small smile.

Back in their unit, Frank, and Bill recounted their morning's adventure, still slightly shaken but also finding a strange sort of humour in the entire ordeal.

"Imagine," Frank chuckled, "us, masterminding a heist of 'Knitting for Beginners'!"

Bill adjusted his velvet smoking jacket. "And 'How to Train Your Budgerigar to Speak Mandarin'! The absurdity of it all!"

As they settled back into their familiar routine, the scent of lavender potpourri suddenly seemed much more comforting. The ordeal had been a bizarre and slightly terrifying interlude in their quiet lives.

From now on, they decided, they would be extra vigilant about returning their library books—just in case the Surry Hills Bookworms Brigade decided to branch out into grand theft auto when they become teenagers.

And perhaps, just perhaps, they would invest in some less conspicuous reading material.

No more books with titles that screamed "potential criminal activity."

And definitely no more books about pickled onions.

FIFTY THOUSAND REASONS

The phone shrieked, dragging Bob from his intense staring contest with a stubborn dandelion. He grumbled and snatched the receiver. "Yeah?"

"Robert! You won't believe the monumental screw-up I've just orchestrated!" Eleanor's voice, usually crisp enough to cut diamonds, was a panicked warble.

Bob sighed. "Let me guess. You've accidentally dyed the cat blue again?"

"Worse! Infinitely worse! Remember that fifty thousand I was transferring for Mum's alpaca farm investment?"

Bob's dandelion forgotten, he sat bolt upright. "The one you said was 'foolproof' and 'couldn't possibly go wrong'?"

"That very one! Well, guess who now has an extra fifty grand jiggling merrily in their bank account?"

Bob blinked. "Don't tell me…"

"Oh, I will tell you! Meant to hit 'E. Peterson, Alpaca Emporium,' fat-fingered 'R. Peterson, Ex-Husband Extraordinaire' instead!" Her dramatic flair, even in crisis, was vintage Eleanor.

A slow grin spread across Bob's face. "So, you're saying I'm currently richer than I've been since that ill-fated investment in inflatable garden gnomes?"

"Don't get any ideas, Robert! This is a disaster! Mum's going to have a llama-fit!"

"A llama-fit?" Bob chuckled. "Is that worse than a hissy fit?"

"It involves more spitting and significantly less coherent yelling. Look, the bank is being about as helpful as a chocolate teapot. Can you just… not spend it on, I don't know, a lifetime supply of those questionable Hawaiian shirts you used to favour?"

"Hey! Those shirts were statements!" Bob protested, though he had to admit they'd been sartorial disasters. "But alright, alright. The fifty thousand is safe with me. Think of it as… temporary alimony, with interest accruing in the form of my amusement."

"Oh, you're finding this funny, are you?" Eleanor's tone sharpened. "Just transfer it back, Bob. And try not to picture yourself as some kind of unexpected lottery winner."

"Consider it done. Though I did briefly consider buying a small island and naming it 'Ex-Wife Estates.'"

A sigh that could curdle milk travelled down the phone line. "Just send the money, Robert."

"Will do, Eleanor. And hey," Bob added, a mischievous glint in his eye, "maybe this is a sign. A sign we should get back together. Think of the financial chaos we could unleash!"

There was a beat of silence. Then, a dry, almost impressed chuckle. "You always were a feisty one, Robert. Just send the money."

THE GHOST WITH GREASE ON HIS HANDS

There's something uniquely terrifying about a ghost with a specific, yet utterly baffling, characteristic.

Most ghosts, you see, opt for the classic "chilling an already cold room" or "whispering your deepest fears into your ear" schtick.

Not Sir Reginald.

Oh no, Sir Reginald preferred the subtle, yet deeply unsettling, approach of leaving grease stains on everything he touched.

I, Bartholomew "Barty" Butterfield, connoisseur of fine napping and purveyor of questionable life choices, inherited Blackwood Manor from my eccentric Aunt Mildred.

The "manor" was less "Downton Abbey" and more "dilapidated shed with delusions of grandeur." I mean, we are talking Northport New South Wales, not Potts Point. Even so, it was mine, and more importantly, it was free. I figured the worst I'd encounter was a few disgruntled possums or a persistent draft.

I was wrong.

Terribly, hilariously wrong.

My first clue that something was amiss wasn't a bloodcurdling scream or a spectral moan.

It was a greasy fingerprint on my freshly laundered tea towel. Now, I'm a bachelor, and my culinary skills extend to reheating pizza, so I knew it wasn't me. I blamed the possums. Those furry little fiends are always up to something.

The next morning, my toothbrush felt… slick.

I mean, not just a little damp from the toothpaste, but like it had been dipped in a vat of industrial-grade lubricant. I gagged, rinsed, and blamed the cheap bristles. Clearly, Blackwood Manor was trying to tell me something about my oral hygiene habits.

But then the grease started appearing with a frequency that defied all logic and sanitation. My remote control developed a sheen that made it feel like a slippery fish. My bedsheets, despite being changed weekly (don't judge, it's progress!), would occasionally sport a perfectly outlined handprint, as if someone had just finished a messy deep-fry session and then patted my pillow.

"This," I declared to my reflection, which looked increasingly haggard, "is not normal possum behaviour."

I started setting up traps.

Not for possums, mind you, but for whatever greasy fiend was invading my personal space. Flour on the floorboards (hoping for footprints, got smear marks). Talcum powder on doorknobs (hoping for clear impressions—got smudges that looked like someone had tried to clean a chimney with their bare hands).

One night, I woke up to a faint clanking sound from the kitchen. My heart, normally a placid goldfish, started doing the Macarena. Armed with a broom (because what else do you use against the unknown?), I tiptoed downstairs. The clanking intensified. I peeked around the doorframe.

There, hovering inches above my ancient, perpetually grimy stove, was a translucent, shimmering figure.

He wasn't particularly menacing.

In fact, he looked rather put-out. And his hands, oh, his hands, were positively glistening.

He was trying to light the stove. Or rather, he was trying to light the stove with a match that kept slipping from his greasy fingers. Each clank was the matchbox falling onto the burner.

"Excuse me!" I squeaked, startling myself as much as the spectral chef.

The ghost spun around, his translucent eyes wide with surprise. He looked like he'd been caught with his hand in the ethereal cookie jar.

"Oh! Good heavens, a living one!" he exclaimed, his voice a faint, reedy whisper that sounded like a rusty hinge. "Didn't think anyone would ever live in this old pile of bricks again. Too much… character."

He gestured vaguely at the peeling wallpaper, and a fresh grease stain appeared on the wall beside him.

"You're the ghost with the grease problem, aren't you?" I asked, lowering my broom. It felt absurd to threaten a spectral entity with a cleaning implement.

He sighed, a faint gust of stale air that smelled faintly of burnt toast.

"Sir Reginald Fitzwilliam, at your service. And yes, I'm afraid I am cursed with this affliction." He held up his hands, which shimmered with an almost iridescent sheen. "It's quite vexing, you know. Can't enjoy a good poltergeist session without leaving a mess. The ectoplasm is one thing, but the grease? Positively uncouth."

I stared at him. "You're a ghost. How do you even get grease on your hands?"

Sir Reginald floated closer, his spectral form causing the surrounding air to feel oddly viscous. "Ah, well, that's the tragedy, my dear fellow. In life, I was a renowned gourmet chef. The finest butter, the richest cream, the most succulent cuts of meat… my hands were always immersed in the very essence of culinary delight. And then… the great goose fat incident."

He paused dramatically, allowing me to imagine some epic culinary disaster.

"I was rendering goose fat, you see, for a challenging confit. A rogue spark, a flimsy apron, and… poof! My corporeal form, alas, was no more. But my spirit, my passion for the culinary arts it lingered. And with it, the very essence of that goose fat. It's infused into my ethereal being."

He looked genuinely mournful.

"Imagine the indignity! I can't even haunt properly. I tried to possess a teacup once, just for a bit of a jape, and the unfortunate thing ended up so greasy, no one would dare drink from it. My spectral touch leaves a tangible, very un-spectral residue."

"So, you're trying to cook?" I asked, pointing to the stove.

"Indeed!" he brightened slightly, though the grease on his hands seemed to intensify. "I simply crave the act of creation. The sizzle, the aroma, the… oh, bother! Another match!"

He dropped the matchbox again, and it slid across the grimy stove top, leaving a trail of shimmering grease.

"Look, Sir Reginald," I began, "I appreciate your passion, but you're making a right mess of my kitchen. Not to mention my toothbrush."

He winced. "My sincerest apologies! It's just this house. It feels like home, in a peculiar, slightly dusty way. And the kitchen it calls to me."

I sighed. A ghost with a culinary obsession and a severe grease problem. This was going to be a long haunting.

"Tell you what," I proposed, "how about we make a deal? You help me clean up all this residue, and in return, I'll let you 'cook' with me. As long as you don't actually touch anything and just offer spectral advice."

"A culinary collaboration? With a living, breathing human? Oh, the possibilities! We could innovate! We could create dishes that transcend the physical plane!"

And so began my unusual cohabitation with Sir Reginald, the greasiest ghost in all of New South Wales.

Our "cooking" sessions were less about actual cooking and more about me fumbling with ingredients while Sir Reginald floated beside me, his translucent hands making intricate gestures that left faint, shimmering trails in the air.

"A touch more paprika, Barty! Infuse it with the passion of a thousand setting suns!" he'd whisper, and a tiny, almost imperceptible grease smudge would appear on the spice jar.

Cleaning became a daily ritual.

He'd hover over the greasy surfaces, his spectral form absorbing some of the residue (though never quite enough). We developed a system: he'd point out the greasiest spots with a dramatic flourish, and I'd follow up with a sponge and a muttered curse.

Life at Blackwood Manor was still a bit messy, but it was also surprisingly less lonely. I had a spectral housemate who gave surprisingly good (though occasionally overly dramatic) cooking advice.

And while I still occasionally found a ghostly grease print on my toast, at least now I knew who to blame. And sometimes, just sometimes, if I left a particularly delicious dish out overnight, I'd wake up to find a tiny, satisfied, grease-free sigh echoing through the manor.

It was his way of saying, "Bravo, Barty. Bravo."

And it made the never-ending battle against the grease almost, almost worth it.

THE CASE OF THE CONTAMINATED COMPOST

I'd always considered Aunt Mildred to be a force of nature. Not a gentle, babbling brook sort of force, mind you.

More like a big cyclone in sensible shoes. She was the kind of woman who believed in tough love, good health food, and the absolute moral superiority of a well-maintained compost heap. So, when she called me, Bartholomew "Barty" Butterfield, in a tone usually reserved for natural disasters or a stubborn weed in her garden, I knew something truly monumental had occurred.

"Barty," she screamed, her voice like a rusty gate hinge amplified by a megaphone. "Get over here. Now. It's an abomination!"

I braced myself. Aunt Mildred's "abominations" ranged from a single plastic bag sorted into the wrong recycling bin to my questionable life choices. Still, the urgency in her voice was new. I imagined a rogue mouse had set up a meth lab in her prize-winning azalea patch, or perhaps someone had dared to suggest putting plastic in the organic waste bin.

I arrived at her cottage, a quaint little dwelling that smelled perpetually of lavender and righteous indignation, to find her standing beside the compost heap. Not on it, mind you, but beside it, as if the very air around it was contaminated.

Her face, usually a roadmap of cheerful wrinkles, was a mask of horror.

Her hands, usually covered in gardening gloves or the flour from her bread baking, were clasped to her chest, trembling slightly.

"Aunt Mildred, what in the name of all that is compostable, is wrong?" I asked, eyeing the steaming pile of organic matter.

It looked perfectly normal to me.

A healthy mix of vegetable scraps, grass clippings, and the occasional rogue tea bag. A faint whiff of earthy decomposition hung in the air, a scent Aunt Mildred usually described as "the sweet perfume of nature's tireless work."

She pointed a trembling, soil-stained finger at the heap. "There," she whispered, as if the compost itself might be listening. "In the very heart of nature's bounty. A weapon."

I squinted.

All I saw was a half-rotted banana peel, a wilting lettuce leaf, and what looked like a particularly robust earthworm.

"A weapon, Aunt Mildred? Did a mouse bring in a tiny, aggressive morsel or has the spirit of a disgruntled potato peel finally risen?"

She let out a sound somewhere between a gasp and a choke, a noise that suggested I had utterly missed the point.

"No, Bartholomew! A gun! A firearm! In my compost! The sheer audacity! The environmental disregard! The unholy metallic presence amongst my nitrogen-rich greens and carbon heavy browns!"

My jaw dropped. A gun? In Aunt Mildred's compost heap?

That was less "rogue mouse meth lab," and more "episode of Midsomer Murders set in a very well-irrigated, morally upright garden."

I cautiously approached the heap. Aunt Mildred took a step back, as if the very presence of the gun might make it spontaneously combust or, worse, become genetically modified. After a moment of rummaging with a trowel, because one does not simply plunge bare hands into Aunt Mildred's compost without proper tools, lest one disturb the delicate microbial balance, I found it.

It was, indeed, a gun.

Not a gleaming, futuristic weapon, but an old, rusty revolver, caked in what appeared to be a mix of decomposed cabbage and what I sincerely hoped was just mud. Its metallic sheen was dulled by organic decay, giving it an oddly rustic, almost natural, appearance.

"Well, I'll be," I muttered, carefully extracting it.

It felt surprisingly heavy, even through the layers of organic decay.

The grip was slimy.

Aunt Mildred gasped again, clutching her chest as if she'd just witnessed a raw chicken being put in a plastic bag.

"Don't touch it, Bartholomew! It's unnatural! It violates the natural order! Who would put such a thing in a compost heap? It's not biodegradable! It's an insult to worms everywhere! Imagine the digestive distress of a beetle trying to break that down!"

Her indignation, as always, was multi-layered.

It wasn't just the criminality of the gun; it was the sheer ecological faux pas. The thought of a non-organic item infiltrating her sacred pile was a deeper offense than any potential murder plot.

"We should call the police, Aunt Mildred," I suggested, holding the gun away from me as if it might sprout tentacles and demand I join a militia.

"The police?" she scoffed, though she still looked utterly horrified. "And tell them what, Bartholomew? That someone has desecrated my carefully curated organic waste? That my worm farm has been tainted by the instruments of violence? They'll think I've finally lost my marbles! And what if it's radioactive? Or worse, non-GMO?"

She squinted at the gun, as if expecting it to glow with an unnatural, inorganic light. Aunt Mildred had a healthy distrust of anything not directly derived from the earth and certainly anything that interfered with the delicate balance of her gut flora.

"It's probably just an old gun, Aunt Mildred," I tried to reassure her. "Someone probably just dumped it there."

"Dumped it?" Her voice rose to a crescendo. "In my compost heap? The very sanctuary of decomposition? The audacity! The unmitigated gall! It's an affront to my compost; it's an affront to me; it's an affront to every organic molecule on this property! What would the tomatoes think? They rely on that soil!"

I refrained from pointing out that the tomatoes currently growing in her greenhouse were probably more concerned with aphids than with the moral implications of firearms.

"Well, we can't just leave it there," I said, putting the gun carefully on a piece of old newspaper, trying to avoid contact with anything other than the paper.

"No, of course not!" she declared, pacing furiously around the compost heap, kicking up little clouds of earthy dust. "It's a blot on the landscape! It's an eyesore! It's a metallurgical anomaly in my biodiverse ecosystem! It's disrupting the fungal networks!"

She then stopped dead, a strange glint in her eye. The horror was slowly being replaced by something else: determination. The same steely resolve she used to conquer stubborn weeds or convince reluctant neighbours to adopt composting. The glint of a woman about to embark on a crusade.

"Bartholomew," she said, her voice now calm yet filled with an ominous resolve. "We need to investigate."

My heart sank.

"Investigate? Aunt Mildred, this isn't a knitting circle mystery. This is a potentially criminal object. It requires forensics, not, well, whatever it is you're thinking."

"Nonsense!" she waved a dismissive hand wave.

"This is my compost heap. And if someone is audacious enough to taint my composting efforts, then I have a right, nay, a duty, to uncover the truth. I am going to find the answers, then I would give them a stern talking to about proper waste disposal and the vital role of lignin decomposition."

The "stern talking to" sounded more terrifying than the gun itself.

And so, for the next few days, our lives revolved around the "Compost Gun Mystery."

Aunt Mildred became a rural Sherlock Holmes, only instead of a deerstalker, she wore a wide-brimmed straw hat, and her magnifying glass was her reading spectacles perpetually perched on her nose. She traded pipe tobacco for a soothing herbal tea, which she'd sip thoughtfully while staring at the gun.

She interviewed the postie, who looked utterly bewildered when asked about suspicious deliveries of "non organic matter." She interrogated Ms Henderson next door, who was only concerned about her prize-winning fuchsias and denied any knowledge of "unusual soil disturbances." She even cross-examined the local magpies, convinced they held some avian secret, perhaps having dropped the gun themselves.

"They're always in the compost, Barty!" she'd insist, pointing a finger at a particularly fat magpie eyeing a discarded apple core. "Perhaps they saw something! They're intelligent birds, you know. Highly observant! And they have a penchant for shiny objects, even rusty ones!"

I spent my days trying to discreetly contact the local police without Aunt Mildred knowing, fearing a lecture on my lack of faith in her investigative prowess or, worse, a demand that I explain the concept of carbon-to-nitrogen ratios to the bewildered constable. The gun, meanwhile, sat on her patio table, an increasingly rusty and incongruous centrepiece that Aunt Mildred periodically sniffed, trying to deduce its origin.

One afternoon, I caught her sprinkling what looked like flour around the gun, meticulously brushing it with a tiny, delicate paintbrush she usually reserved for dusting her porcelain figurines.

"Aunt Mildred, what are you doing?" I asked, exasperated.

"Dusting for prints, Bartholomew!" she declared, as if it were the most natural thing in the world. "One must be thorough. Though I suspect any fingerprints would be terribly organic by now. Perhaps we'll find a carbon imprint! Or evidence of trace elements from a misguided fertiliser."

She paused, then added, "It makes me wonder, though. What sort of villain would choose a compost heap? It's so uncivilised. And the smell! Imagine trying to make a quick getaway with the lingering aroma of decaying vegetables on your person. It simply lacks a certain panache."

She shuddered.

Clearly, the aesthetic offense of the compost-buried gun was as bad, if not worse, than its criminal implications.

In the end, the mystery was solved not by Aunt Mildred's "organic forensics" but by a rather sheepish-looking young man from the town.

He'd come to Aunt Mildred's, red-faced and stammering, admitting that he'd "accidentally" dropped his grandfather's old, defunct relic of a revolver into the compost heap while trying to dispose of it "responsibly" and out of sight. He thought the heat of the compost would somehow make it disappear, a bizarre form of nature-assisted evidence destruction. He was, apparently, less interested in gun safety and more interested in avoiding a stern lecture from his own grandmother about clutter.

Aunt Mildred listened to his confession with a raised eyebrow, her arms crossed, her eyes narrowed. When he finished, she simply nodded.

"I see," she said, her voice deceptively mild. "So, you believe my compost heap is a suitable repository for firearms, do you? You think my carefully nurtured microorganisms are simply there to assist in the disposal of your misguided attempts at whatever that was? You assume my beneficial bacteria are a clean-up crew for your irresponsibility?"

The young man visibly paled, taking a step back as if Aunt Mildred herself might spontaneously combust with righteous indignation.

"Now," Aunt Mildred continued, her voice gaining momentum, "I want you to go home, young man. And I want you to research the proper, environmentally sound methods of disposing of such an item. And then, I want you to write me a ten-page essay on the importance of responsible waste management and the dangers of improper metallic disposal in organic matter, citing at least three academic sources. And I want it by Friday. Double-spaced."

He practically fled, muttering apologies, no doubt envisioning an entire weekend spent poring over Environment Protection Australia guidelines for hazardous waste.

Aunt Mildred then turned to me, a smug, satisfied look on her face. "You see, Bartholomew? I found the underlying cause of the issue, and I made sure the culprit learnt a valuable lesson. Now, help me move this thing to the shed. I need to turn the compost; it's looking sluggish. And perhaps you can help me find a non-toxic rust remover. For the trowel, of course."

And just like that, the Compost Gun Mystery was over, replaced by the more pressing matter of compost aeration.

Life with Aunt Mildred, I reflected, was never dull.

And somewhere out there, a young man was probably regretting every single one of his compost-related decisions, now forever burdened with the knowledge of proper metallurgical disposal.

THE GREAT HONEY HEIST

Barry and Barnaby were not your average sun bears. Oh sure, they enjoyed favouring fruits, insects, small animals, and an afternoon nap in a sunbeam, just like any self-respecting Ursus arctos. But beneath their shaggy sun coats beat the hearts of true culinary connoisseurs, specifically when it came to the golden, viscous nectar known as honey. And for two years, their existence at Taronga Zoo had been a cruel, honey-less torment.

Their pen, a marvel of modern zoological engineering, was designed to keep bears in. It had high electric fences, reinforced concrete walls, and a moat filled with... well, it was mostly just stagnant water, but the threat of a moat was there. What the engineers hadn't accounted for, however, were two bears with an intellect honed by years of strategic honey deprivation.

"Barnaby," Barry rumbled one Tuesday morning, nudging a loose rock with his snout. "I've had it. I dreamt of eucalyptus honey last night. Raw, unfiltered, still got the little bee legs in it. It was glorious."

Barnaby, usually the more reserved of the two, let out a deep sigh that rattled the leaves on a nearby tree. "Don't even talk about it, Barry. My salivary glands are revolting. Remember that sliver of comb old Mildred the zookeeper accidentally dropped last spring? I still taste it in my dreams."

"I know, mate. Let execute our plan."

"Right-o."

Their escape plan had been meticulously, if slowly, formulated. It involved the aforementioned loose rock, a cleverly timed distraction (a particularly loud sneeze from Barnaby usually did the trick, startling the less vigilant interns), and a dash of pure, unadulterated bear audacity.

The rock, over months of patient nudging and strategic pawing, had become a perfect fulcrum against a weak spot in the fence line. Today was the day.

"Alright, Barnaby, on three," Barry whispered, his eyes glinting with mischievous delight. "One... two... ACHOO!"

Barnaby delivered a sneeze of epic proportions, a guttural expulsion of air and bear snot that echoed across the zoo grounds. A new intern, still blinking away sleep, nearly dropped his bucket of primate chow. It was enough.

Barry, with a surprising burst of agility for a creature of his bulk, jammed the rock into the pre-weakened section of the fence. With a groan of tortured metal, the wire sprang outwards, creating a gap just wide enough for a determined bear.

"Go, go, go!" Barry urged, already squeezing through. Barnaby, less graceful but equally motivated, followed with a shimmy that would have made a professional contortionist proud.

They were out. Free. And more importantly, hungry for honey.

Their destination was no secret. Every zookeeper knew that the Honey Stash, a veritable Fort Knox of golden goodness, was in the back of the commissary building, behind three locked doors and a sign that read, in stern red letters: "DO NOT ENTER—BEAR PROOF."

Barry and Barnaby took a moment to appreciate the irony.

The journey was a blur of thrilling freedom. They galloped past the bewildered zebras, startling a flock of flamingos into a pink cloud of panic, and even briefly considered liberating the seals and sea lions.

Reaching the commissary, they found the first door ajar. "Beginner's luck," Barry grunted, already sniffing the air. The scent of sweet, sweet honey was growing stronger, intoxicating their senses.

The second door was locked, but Barnaby, with the brute force of a thousand un-honeyed dreams, simply pushed. The wood splintered with a satisfying crack, and the door swung inward.

And then they saw it. The Honey Stash.

It wasn't just a stash; it was an alcove. Jars of eucalyptus honey, yellow box, red box, you name it. It is grown in Australia, that honey was here. A treasure trove. The honeycombs dripping with pure sweetness—stacked from floor to ceiling. The aroma was so potent it made their eyes water.

Barry let out a primal roar of triumph, a sound that sent shivers down the spines of the nearby squirrel population. Barnaby, meanwhile, had already buried his face in a five-kilo bucket of yellow box honey.

It was a beautiful, sticky chaos.

They ripped open jars with their teeth, smeared honey across their faces and paws, and occasionally paused to let out contented grunts of pure bliss. Barry tried to fit an entire honeycomb in his mouth at once, resulting in a comical dribble of sticky gold down his chin.

Barnaby, ever the pragmatist, was attempting to scoop honey directly from a vat with his paws, turning his forelegs into golden, furry clubs.

The sounds of their revelry eventually reached the ears of Mildred, the same zookeeper who had once dropped the fateful sliver of honeycomb. She arrived, broom in hand, to find a scene of utter, delicious devastation.

Two sun bears, now more golden sun than anything else, sat amidst a sea of shattered glass, sticky puddles, and empty honey jars. Their fur was matted with honey, their whiskers dripped with it, and their bellies were distended to an alarming degree.

Mildred, a woman who had seen her fair share of animal antics, simply stared. Then a slow smile spread across her face. She knew, deep down, that this was inevitable.

Barry, still licking the last remnants of a jar, looked up at her, his eyes twinkling. He let out a small, contented burp. Barnaby, slumped against a stack of empty containers, merely offered a blissful groan.

The great honey heist was over.

The bears were sticky, satisfied, and possibly suffering from a severe sugar rush.

Mildred knew she had a monumental cleanup on her hands, but as she looked at the two thrilled, albeit incredibly messy, bears, she couldn't help but chuckle.

"Well," she said, surveying the devastation. "At least you boys had fun. Now, who's going to help me clean this up?"

Barry and Barnaby, in unison, closed their eyes and pretended to be asleep.

Some things, even a mountain of honey, couldn't motivate a bear to do.

THE FIVE WARNINGS OF MOTHERHOOD

"Honestly, Chloe," Sarah declared, pushing a stray, clearly unwashed curl out of her eye, "motherhood should come with a giant, flashing, neon warning label. Not those cute little pamphlets they give you at the hospital that show a serene baby cooing at a perfectly coiffed mother. More like a legally binding, 300-page document filled with disclaimers and testimonials of sleep-deprived horrors."

Chloe, ever the picture of togetherness with her sensible bob and crisp linen shirt, took a dainty sip of her latte. She eyed her best friend across the tiny café table, a mixture of sympathy and mild bewilderment playing on her face.

Sarah, usually vibrant and energetic, currently resembled a startled owl who had just survived a bar brawl. Her t-shirt bore what looked suspiciously like dried oatmeal, and her designer handbag was overflowing with what could only be described as baby-related paraphernalia, including a rogue teether that looked like it had been in a fight with a chew toy.

"It can't be that bad, can it?" Chloe ventured, ever the optimist, or perhaps, the blissfully ignorant. "I mean, little Leo is adorable. All those Instagram photos of him smiling."

Sarah snorted, a sound remarkably similar to a frustrated meerkat.

"Instagram, my dear Chloe, is a highly curated lie. It's the digital equivalent of a Hollywood set where everything off camera is utter pandemonium. For every one of those 'precious moments,' there are twenty-seven where I'm questioning my life choices while covered in a bodily fluid that didn't originate from me."

She leaned in conspiratorially. "Let me give you a glimpse behind the curtain. The first warning label item: 'WARNING: Your Bladder Is No Longer Your Own.' Before Leo, I could hold it for hours. Now, I feel a trickle of liquid, and my pelvic floor does a dramatic reenactment of the Titanic sinking. And don't even get me started on trying to pee alone. I swear, the moment my bottom hits the seat, the baby monitor transforms into a banshee, or a tiny hand snakes under the door, or Leo just appears, staring at me with those wide, innocent eyes, like I'm performing a circus act. Privacy? What's privacy?"

Chloe chuckled, then stopped, realizing Sarah was dead serious. "Okay, okay, point taken. But surely the sleep improves?"

"The sleep?" Sarah repeated, "Ah, yes, the mythical 'sleep.' Warning label number two: 'WARNING: You Will Redefine Exhaustion.' Do you know how people say they're 'tired'? They have no idea. I've reached a new plane of existence where my brain frequently confuses words, and I've almost put the milk in the cupboard and the cereal in the fridge more times than I can count. This morning, I tried to brush my teeth with nipple cream."

Chloe gasped, then clapped a hand over her mouth to stifle a laugh. "No way!"

"Way," Sarah confirmed, nodding grimly.

"And then I tried to put my bra on my head. It's like my brain cells are actively fleeing the scene of the crime. The only thing keeping me upright right now is this lukewarm coffee and the sheer terror of what Leo might dismantle if I actually pass out."

She took a fortifying gulp of her coffee.

"Then there's warning label number three: 'WARNING: Prepare to Lose All Sense of Personal Hygiene and Fashion.' Remember when I used to coordinate my accessories? Now, my accessories are whatever spit-up stain doesn't show up too badly on my darkest t-shirt. My hair? A perpetual 'messy bun' that's more 'bird's nest' than 'chic.' And showers? They're a luxury, Chloe. A full, uninterrupted, hot shower? That's my dream vacation now. Not Fiji, or Phuket, or Bora Bora. Just 15 minutes of steam and soap without a small human attempting to chew on the shower curtain."

Chloe winced. "I noticed you were dressed casually."

"'Casually' is a polite term for 'I wrestled a toddler into his car seat, nearly dislocated my shoulder, and then realised I was still wearing yesterday's yoga pants'," Sarah retorted. "And don't even get me started on social outings. Warning label number four: 'WARNING: Your Social Life Will Shrink to the Size of a Pea.' This, right here, is a monumental achievement. A full hour out of the house! I had to orchestrate it like a military operation, involving three feeds, two diaper changes, one emergency outfit change for Leo (because of projectile vomit), and a frantic search for the pacifier that had mysteriously vanished into the abyss behind the sofa."

She sighed dramatically. "Last week, I tried to go to a playgroup. It was like a gladiatorial arena, but with more snot and judgment. And the conversations! It's all about poop consistency, sleep regressions, and the merits of organic pureed carrots. I miss talking about books, movies, or even just celebrity gossip. Now, my most exciting conversation of the day is debating whether Leo's latest burp was a 'satisfied rumble' or a 'prelude to a spit-up.' riveting stuff."

Chloe giggled. "Okay, I get it. It's different."

"Different is an understatement," Sarah said, then leaned back, a wistful look on her face. "And yet warning label number five: 'WARNING: You Will Experience Unconditional Love So Intense It Might Actually Hurt.' Because despite the projectile vomit, the sleepless nights, the constant anxiety, the loss of personal space, and the nipple cream toothpaste incident he'll flash that gummy smile, or wrap his tiny hand around my finger, or just snuggle into my chest, and suddenly, every single complaint vanishes. Every ounce of exhaustion, every frustrating moment, just melts away. It's like being hit by a tiny, adorable, highly infectious love bomb."

Her eyes softened, and a genuine smile, free from the exhaustion, finally broke through. "And then, just when you think you've got it, when you're utterly saturated in this overwhelming adoration, he'll unleash the most epic diaper explosion known to humanity, usually five minutes before you have to leave the house for that 'monumental achievement' coffee meeting."

Chloe burst out laughing, a full, hearty laugh that made other café customers glance over.

"So, what you're saying is, it's a beautiful, messy, hilarious, terrifying, wonderful, completely unhinged ride?"

"Precisely!" Sarah exclaimed, her own laughter bubbling up. "It's like riding a roller coaster designed by a mad scientist who forgot to include brakes but occasionally throws confetti and kittens at you. And you just have to hang on for dear life. But seriously, someone needs to print that warning label. Stick it on every baby registry. Tattoo it on expectant parents' foreheads. Just… give us a heads-up!"

She picked up a stray baby wipe that had fallen from her bag and absently started cleaning a spill on the table. "At least they could warn you about the sheer volume of wipes you'd go through. Or that you'd develop the ability to function in less sleep than a bat. Or that your vocabulary would suddenly include terms like 'blowout' and 'cluster feeding'."

Chloe, still smiling, reached across the table and patted Sarah's hand.

"Well, you're doing an amazing job, despite the lack of official warnings. And at least you've got stories for days."

"Stories, yes," Sarah agreed, a glint in her eye.

"Horror stories, mostly. But with an unbelievably cute protagonist. Now, if you'll excuse me, I think I just felt a phantom burp on my shoulder, and I need to mentally prepare myself for the next round of glorious, un-warned-about chaos." She gathered her overflowing bag, a tiny sock dangling precariously from the zipper. "See you next month, maybe? If Leo allows it, and if I can remember how to get here."

As Sarah navigated her way out of the café, a tired but resolute warrior, Chloe watched her go, a thoughtful expression on her face. She took another sip of her latte, then paused, a sudden, inexplicable urge to check her own hair for suspicious stains washing over her. Maybe, just maybe, Sarah had a point. A warning label wouldn't be such a bad idea after all. Especially one that mentioned the nipple cream.

THE CASE OF THE FUNKY EAR

I lay sprawled on the sun-warmed kitchen tiles, dreaming of chasing galahs, when I was rudely interrupted by a high pitched, indignant yelp.

"Barnaby! Oh, for the love of Royal Canin food, Barnaby!"

It was Daisy, my sister, a beagle with a nose for trouble. She stood over me, one floppy ear twitching furiously, her tail thumping a rapid, worried rhythm against the floor.

I opened one lazy eye. "What fresh hell hath the mailman wrought now, Daisy?"

"It's not the mailman! It's me!" she declared, nudging her head closer to my nose. "Smell this, Barnaby. Just take a whiff."

Being a beagle, I took a whiff.

My powerful snout, usually a finely tuned instrument for detecting forgotten snacks, wrinkled. I sniffed again, more deeply this time, my nostrils flaring. My jowls rippled.

"By the beard of the great hound in the sky, Daisy, what in the name of all that is holy have you rolled in that has gotten in your ear?"

"Nothing! That's the point!" Daisy wailed, pawing at the offending ear.

"It's just funky! It's got this je ne sais quoi of, well, of funk!"

As a connoisseur of smells both delightful and disgusting, I had to agree. It wasn't the usual delightful aroma of fresh dirt.

This was different.

This was a deep, resonant funk.

"It's almost musical. Like a jazz solo played by an old damp sock," I mused.

"Don't be ridiculous! It's embarrassing! What if the human smells it?" Daisy snapped.

"You cavorted with that brown marmorated stink bug last Tuesday," I reminded her.

"That's beside the point! This is internal funk! It's coming from me! I'm a funky beagle, Barnaby! My life is over! No more belly rubs! No more chasing butterflies! I'll be exiled to the land of the perpetually unsniffable!"

I sighed.

I leant in, giving the ear another, more investigative sniff.

"Hmm. It's got notes of a stale biscuit. Is that optimistic?"

Daisy looked up. "Optimism?"

"Yes! It's not just funky, Daisy. It's artisan funky. It's unique. It's you."

"So, I'm not just funky? I'm artistically funky?"

"Precisely. Now, if you'll excuse me, I believe I smell a very faint, very distant, and potentially very funky discarded hot dog wrapper. Duty calls."

And with that, I trotted off, leaving Daisy to contemplate the artistic merits of her own unique funk, a faint smile on her jowly face.

PHANTOM FUNDS

It was a Tuesday afternoon which, in the office of Artistic Follies Pty Ltd (our creatively named graphic design firm), usually meant a mild existential dread followed by the consumption of lukewarm afternoon coffee. This particular Tuesday, however, was different. This Tuesday, the air hummed with a peculiar blend of anticipation and, well, sparkle.

Our esteemed boss, Mr Henderson, a man whose sartorial choices often reflected the state of his digestive system (beige on good days, plaid on Tuesdays), had just introduced us to our new accountant, Ms Felicity Featherstone.

Now, let's be frank. Mr Henderson was not known for his discerning eye for hiring based on anything other than a candidate's ability to operate a stapler. Yet, Felicity was different.

She wasn't just attractive; she was the kind of attractive that made you wonder if she had a personal wind machine following her around, ensuring her auburn curls always caught the light just so.

Her smile could disarm a bank vault, and her eyes, the colour of warm caramel, seemed to twinkle with an almost supernatural understanding of well, numbers, apparently.

"Team," Mr Henderson had announced, his usual nervous twitch momentarily subdued, "this is Felicity. She'll be taking over our financials. Felicity, meet the creative team." He gestured vaguely at our motley crew, who collectively looked like they'd just been caught sneaking cookies from the break room.

We nodded, mumbled greetings, and promptly went back to staring at our computer screens, pretending to be busy. But secretly, every single one of us, from Brenda in layout to Gary, our resident coffee-stained web designer, was thinking the same thing: Wow. What a beauty!

And here's the kicker: Felicity wasn't just a pretty face.

She was, as it turned out, an accounting savant.

She organised our chaotic ledger system with the precision of a Swiss watchmaker.

She found discrepancies we didn't even know existed (mostly involving Gary's "business expenses" for exotic cat food). She even got old 'Grumpy Jenkins' from 'Jenkins & Sons Mortuary Supplies' to pay his overdue invoice, a feat previously considered impossible.

"She's a miracle worker!" Mr. Henderson crowed one afternoon, beaming as Felicity presented him with a meticulously colour-coded report. "Felicity, you've streamlined everything!"

And she had.

Perhaps too much.

It started innocently enough.

One rainy Friday, Felicity had a sudden, urgent need for funds.

A "dire personal emergency," she'd vaguely explained to the empty office. Something about a rare, imported artisanal cheese subscription that absolutely had to be paid by 5 PM or her life in the kitchen would lose all meaning. Being the diligent accountant, she was, and with no one else around, she simply 'borrowed' from the company.

A somewhat inconsiderable sum.

Not enough to raise immediate flags, but enough to cover the cheese and perhaps a small, emergency truffle.

Monday morning, bright and early, a peculiar thing happened.

Felicity's next pay cheque landed in her account, and almost immediately, an equivalent amount (plus a thoughtful 0.5% "administrative fee" she silently charged herself) pinged its way back into the company's primary account.

Seamless.

Undetected.

And, crucially, repaid.

A small, delighted shiver ran down Felicity's spine.

It was so easy. Nobody knew. Nobody questioned.

The system, her beautiful, perfectly organised system, was her oyster.

The artisanal cheese incident was, in retrospect, merely a test flight.

The real borrowing began not too long after.

A slightly larger sum this time, for a 'much-needed therapeutic weekend retreat' to recover from the stress of perfectly balancing Artistic Follies's books.

This time, the repayment didn't happen.

Or rather, it happened in a more abstract sense.

It was absorbed into the general ebb and flow of receivables, a phantom client payment, a 'miscellaneous income' entry that only Felicity's genius mind could conjure.

This went on for several years.

Felicity, with her serene smile, fantastic looks, and impeccable spreadsheets, continued to be the company's financial guardian angel. She meticulously managed the books, always making sure there was just enough in the coffers to cover payroll, rent, and Mr Henderson's increasingly frequent stress induced bulk orders of camomile tea.

The rest of us, the 'team,' were none the wiser.

When bonus season rolled around, and the usual hefty envelopes were replaced by a crisp twenty-dollar note and a polite suggestion to enjoy a celebratory beverage, we just shrugged.

"Must be a tough year," we'd murmur to each other.

"Clients aren't paying their invoices, eh?"

This was, unfortunately, a common lament in our line of work.

People love pretty designs, but paying for them? That's a different story.

Christmas gifts, which had once been extravagant hampers filled with artisanal chocolates and questionable fruitcakes, dwindled to a single, slightly bruised satsuma and a sincere handshake.

Mr Henderson, whose wardrobe had regressed almost entirely to various shades of grey, seemed to be perpetually wearing a worried frown that could curdle milk. He'd pace the office, muttering about 'cash flow' and "unforeseen expenses." We just assumed the wider world did not appreciate our art enough.

Then came the bombshell.

Felicity, our brilliant, beautiful, indispensable Felicity, announced she was quitting.

Moving away.

To a "private island with excellent tax incentives," she'd chirped, her eyes twinkling even more brightly than usual showing a selfie of herself in a tiny bikini she was going to wear on the private beach of a house she purchased.

A collective gasp rippled through the office.

How would we survive without her?

Who would untangle Gary's expenses now?

Mr Henderson, however, saw an opportunity.

A final, grand gesture before Felicity's departure. "Felicity," he declared, "as a farewell, and to ensure a smooth transition, I've asked our former accountant, Mr Higgins, to come in and do a final audit. Just a formality, you understand."

Felicity's smile didn't waver, but if you listened closely, you might have heard the faintest, almost imperceptible clink of alarm bells ringing in her caramel-coloured eyes.

Mr Higgins arrived, a stoic, bespectacled man whose personality was as beige as Mr Henderson's preferred trousers. He brought with him a battered briefcase, a lifetime's worth of cynicism, and a calculator that looked like it had survived the invention of electricity.

Felicity, ever the professional, offered to sit with him, to "assist" with the audit. Mr Henderson, ever the trusting soul, agreed. And so, the strangest week in Artistic Follies's history began.

Night after night, the lights in Felicity's glass-walled office burned late.

You could see Mr Higgins hunched over the ledgers, his bald head gleaming under the fluorescent lights, a tiny frown deepening with each turn of a page. And there, beside him, was Felicity, perched elegantly, offering "clarifications" and "contextual insights" that, to our untrained ears, sounded like she was describing the migratory patterns of obscure Amazonian butterflies.

The atmosphere in the rest of the office was electric.

We pretended to work, but every few minutes, someone would "accidentally" wander past Felicity's office, craning their neck for a glimpse. We watched Mr Higgins's frown deepen, his movements becoming more agitated. We saw him hold up checks to the light, muttering to himself.

One evening, Brenda swore she saw him pull out a magnifying glass and sniff a ledger, as if trying to detect the faint scent of missing zeroes. Gary, ever the pragmatist, started a betting pool on how many "un-deposited" checks Mr Higgins would find. The odds favoured "more than twenty."

Then came the morning of Felicity's last day.

Mr Higgins emerged from the office, looking like he'd just wrestled a spreadsheet monster. He marched straight to Mr Henderson's office; his calculator clutched like a weapon. The door closed, but the muffled shouts and occasional thud of a fist hitting a desk were clear.

Felicity, meanwhile, was packing her desk. She whistled a jaunty tune, oblivious (or so she seemed) to the storm brewing. Her "private island" looked like it was calling.

When Mr Henderson finally emerged, he was a shade of reddish brown that clashed terribly with his plaid shirt. He strode to Felicity's office, his face a mask of bewildered fury. He didn't shout. He didn't even raise his voice. He simply pointed a trembling finger at a pile of documents Mr Higgins had meticulously stacked.

"Felicity," he said, his voice barely a whisper, "these are your pay stubs. It appears you were paying yourself twice. And sometimes thrice. And occasionally, five times."

Felicity, bless her cotton socks, simply smiled.

A serene smile.

"Oh, Mr Henderson," she purred, "it seems you've stumbled upon my unique, highly efficient, and entirely secret 'Advanced Cash Flow Optimization' system. It's revolutionary, really. Very cutting edge."

Mr Henderson stared at her, his jaw slack. The "Advanced Cash Flow Optimization" system, it turned out, primarily involved optimizing the flow of cash directly into Felicity's personal accounts. She wasn't simply good at her job; she was a criminal mastermind disguised as an angel.

The police arrived shortly after.

Felicity, still smiling, still looking impossibly glamorous, was escorted out, her "private island" plans likely put on hold for a considerably less private, New South Wales funded accommodation.

It was an interesting time to work at Artistic Follies.

We didn't get our bonuses back, nor our Christmas hams.

But we did get a hell of a story, and a renewed appreciation for accountants who weren't so optimistic with their cash flow.

Mr Henderson, in his next hiring round, insisted on candidates who looked definitively less like supermodels and more like they had a deep, personal relationship with a ledger.

Just to be safe.

A DELICIOUS REWARD

Mortimer was a perfectly respectable rodent. He had a neat little burrow under the floorboards of Ms Higgins's pantry, a well-organised collection of crumbs, and an impressive ability to blush even under his fur. His shyness was legendary amongst the local mouse community. He once tried to ask for a piece of discarded cracker from Bartholomew, the boisterous barn mouse, and ended up stammering so much he accidentally offered Bartholomew his own prize-winning raisin.

His biggest challenge, however, was the weekly Cheese Day.

Every Tuesday, Ms Higgins would bring home a new, gloriously pungent block of cheddar, Gruyère, or, on truly magnificent occasions, a crumbly Stilton. For Mortimer, this was both a dream and a nightmare. The scent alone was enough to make his whiskers twitch with desire, but the thought of venturing out into the vast, echoing kitchen, potentially encountering a human foot or, worse, Ms Higgins's terrifyingly fluffy cat, Mittens, filled him with existential dread.

One Tuesday, the aroma was particularly intoxicating. It was a mature cheddar, sharp and inviting. Mortimer's stomach rumbled a protest that echoed through his tiny burrow. He paced; he wrung his tiny paws. He even tried to convince a dust bunny to go instead (it politely declined, citing prior engagements).

Finally, driven by a hunger he couldn't ignore, Mortimer took a deep breath. "Just a quick dash," he whispered to himself, his voice barely audible even to his own ears. "In and out. Like a ninja mouse. An incredibly nervous ninja mouse."

He scurried out from under the floorboards, his heart pounding like a drum solo. The kitchen seemed enormous, the refrigerator a towering white cliff, the table a distant, perilous plateau. And there, on the counter, was the cheese. A golden beacon of deliciousness.

Mortimer crept along the baseboards, using the shadows as his cloak. He reached the leg of the counter, a sheer climb for a mouse of his delicate constitution. He ascended, one tiny claw after another, muttering encouragement to himself. "You can do it, Mortimer! Think of the cheese! Think of not being hungry!"

He was halfway up when disaster struck.

Mittens stretched languidly on the kitchen rug, let out a massive yawn, and then, with the casual indifference of a feline overlord, began to groom her paw. Her tail, thick and luxurious, twitched. And twitched. Right across Mortimer's path.

Mortimer froze.

He was eye-level with a single, fluffy, twitching cat tail. His shyness, combined with sheer panic, caused an unprecedented reaction. He didn't scream. He didn't run. He fainted.

He plummeted a mere two inches, landing with a soft thud on the rug directly beneath Mittens' twitching tail.

Mittens, startled by the unexpected thud, opened one golden eye. She peered down, sniffed once, and then, with a sigh that seemed to convey the immense burden of being a cat, simply stepped over him and continued her grooming. She hadn't even registered him as a mouse, merely an inconvenient lump.

Mortimer came to, dazed, moments later.

He looked up at the retreating fluffy rear of Mittens, then at the towering counter, then back at his tiny, trembling paws.

He had fainted.

Over a tail.

He was, quite possibly, the most pathetic mouse in the history of mice.

But then he noticed something.

Just beside where he'd landed, a tiny, perfect crumb of cheddar had fallen from the counter.

It was small, but it was there.

And it was his.

Mortimer carefully nudged the crumb with his nose. Then, with a renewed sense of purpose, he dragged his prize back to his burrow.

He might be shy, he might faint at the sight of a cat's tail, but he had faced his fears (sort of), and he had returned victorious.

And the cheese, oh, the cheese, was glorious.

He decided then and there that sometimes, the best way to conquer your fears was to just accidentally fall into a delicious reward.

THE PURSUIT OF PARROT PROPULSION

The afternoon sun, as golden and syrupy as Manuka honey, dripped through the ancient Rātā trees of Whenua Hou, painting dappled patterns on the forest floor. Kevin, a Kakapo parrot of impressive girth and even more impressive vocal cords (capable of a boom that could shake dew from a fern), let out a sigh that rustled the surrounding flax bushes. Beside him, Steve, equally rotund but with a perpetually bewildered glint in his lime-green eyes, was attempting to dislodge a stubborn berry from a low-hanging branch.

"Just a little further," Steve grunted, his foot slipping. He tumbled backward into a pile of damp leaves with a soft thump. "Blast it all! If only this blasted branch were a smidgen lower. Or if I were… taller."

Kevin squinted, a knowing glint in his own round, yellow eyes. "Or if we could fly, Steve. Like literally every other feathered creature in this entire land, save for our distant kiwi cousins and those rather ostentatious emu imports."

Steve pulled himself upright, a leaf clinging to his beak like a tiny green moustache. "Don't even start, Kev. It's a sore subject. Just yesterday, I saw a fantail—a bird barely bigger than my eyeball—flitting about, mocking me with its aerial acrobatics. It even did a little loop-de-loop. A loop-de-loop, Kevin!"

"And don't forget that kererū that dive-bombed poor Brenda's prize kumara patch," Kevin added, shuddering.

"The sheer audacity! Imagine, Steve, soaring over the canopy, picking out the juiciest berries, or perhaps, just perhaps, escaping a stoat with dignity instead of having to waddle like a fluffy, emerald bowling ball."

The thought of dignified escape clearly appealed to Steve. He preened a bit, ruffling his already dishevelled feathers. "A majestic ascent, followed by a graceful, albeit rapid, descent onto a fresh patch of tender shoots. No more huffing and puffing up hills. No more strategically placed rocks to jump from, only to misjudge the distance and end up in a ditch."

"Or needing to be airlifted to safety by humans wearing funny hats," Kevin muttered, recalling an embarrassing incident during a conservation check-up. "The sheer indignity."

They sat in thoughtful silence, the injustice of their grounded existence weighing heavily on their considerable frames. Kakapo, unlike their avian brethren, had evolved a rather unique lifestyle. They were nocturnal masters of camouflage, excellent climbers, and boasted a powerful sense of smell. But flight? A distant, often painful, memory from their evolutionary past. Their wings, vestigial and comically small, were more useful for propping themselves up after an enthusiastic waddle than for generating any discernible lift.

"It just doesn't make sense," Steve pondered aloud, picking at a loose feather. "We have wings. They're just decorative. Like a tiny hat on a very large, green potato."

"Exactly!" Kevin exclaimed, startled. "It's like being given a perfectly good pair of flippers but then being told you're only allowed to swim in molasses. We're built for the air, Steve. I can feel it in my... well, in my incredibly dense bones."

Steve's eyes lit up, not with immediate understanding, but with the dawning of an idea so outlandish it could only be conceived by a Kakapo. "You know, Kevin, I was reading this rather fascinating piece of leaf-mould the other day—had some interesting beetle larvae, too—but it also contained a curious illustration. Two upright creatures, not unlike us, but with even smaller wings, yet they were depicted aloft, in a contraption of wood and canvas."

Kevin blinked. "You're talking about the mythical 'Wright brothers' again, aren't you? The ones the humans jabber about. Blokes who decided gravity was merely a suggestion."

"Precisely!" Steve puffed out his chest, a self-important look on his face. "If those featherless bipeds, with their paltry arm-wings, could figure out how to defy the very laws of nature, then why can't we? We have actual feathers, Kevin! Billions of them!"

Kevin's feathery brow furrowed in thought. The idea, while utterly preposterous, had a certain… irresistible lunacy to it. "So, you're suggesting we… build a flying machine? Out here? With what? More leaves? Sticks? Our own boundless optimism?"

"All of the above!" Steve declared, springing to his feet with an uncharacteristic burst of energy that promptly sent him stumbling again. "Think of it, Kevin! We don't need to flap our own pathetic excuses for wings. We need mechanical wings! Bigger wings! Wings that work!"

And so began the Great Kakapo Aviation Project. Their laboratory was a secluded hollow beneath a giant fern. Their materials were abundant: sturdy twigs became structural beams, large Nikau palm fronds were earmarked for wing surfaces, supple kiekie vines were perfect for lashing, and, of course, their own prodigious shedding provided an endless supply of high-quality, downy insulation, and aerodynamic surfaces.

Their first prototype, affectionately dubbed "The Green Goblin 1.0," was a masterpiece of avian amateur engineering. It comprised two massive palm fronds lashed together with surprising strength, forming a crude biplane. In the middle, a small, woven basket (originally intended for particularly plump grubs) served as the cockpit.

"Alright, Steve," Kevin boomed, adjusting his position in the snug basket. "Remember the principles! Lift, drag, thrust, and… not falling face-first into a nettle patch."

Steve, positioned precariously on a nearby log, held a long stick. "Ready for launch! On the count of three! One… two… THRUST!" He jammed the stick under the contraption, giving it a mighty shove.

The Green Goblin 1.0 lurched forward, wobbled violently, and then, with a pathetic flutter of its frond-wings, tipped gracefully onto its side, sending Kevin tumbling out into a surprisingly soft bed of moss. He emerged covered in green fluff, looking utterly unperturbed.

"Remarkable, Steve," he said, shaking off a large clump. "We achieved sideways momentum. A new frontier in terrestrial travel."

Their next few attempts were equally spectacular failures. "The Feathered Falcon" (a large, somewhat sticky construction of shed feathers and tree sap) barely managed a foot-long skid before disintegrating. "The Vine Vindicator" (an intricate web of woven vines designed to capture wind) merely ensnared a very indignant Wētā.

The local Tūī, perched high in the canopy, often watched their antics with undisguised amusement, occasionally letting out a series of mocking, bell-like calls. Kevin and Steve, however, remained undeterred, fuelled by their shared dream and an endless supply of delicious fern roots.

One crisp morning, after a rigorous design session that involved copious amounts of grunting and head-scratching, Steve presented his magnum opus: "The Great Green Glider." It wasn't a flapping machine, but a streamlined (for a Kakapo) structure of lightweight tree fern trunks, covered meticulously with layers of large, overlapping leaves, all bound with hundreds of meters of painstakingly stripped flax fibre. It even had a tail made of particularly rigid tree fungus for "directional stability."

"The principle, Kevin," Steve explained, puffing out his chest, "is not to fly, per se, but to glide with purpose. We launch from a high point, catch the updraft, and simply sail."

They dragged the cumbersome contraption to the highest point they knew—a gently sloping ridge overlooking a lush patch of their favourite mosses. With a combined effort of much pushing, panting, and not a little grumbling, they positioned The Great Green Glider at the very edge.

"You first, Steve," Kevin insisted, ever the proponent of practical experimentation.

Steve, despite his earlier bravado, hesitated. "Are you sure this is wise, Kevin? The wind, it's… blustery. And that particularly sharp rock down there looks rather… pointy."

"Nonsense!" Kevin declared, giving the glider a helpful shove. "For science! For flight! For not having to waddle through muddy patches!"

With a final push, The Great Green Glider teetered, caught a gust, and then, with a majestic, if slightly wobbly, sweep, it lifted. It didn't soar. It didn't even glide gracefully. But for a glorious two seconds, it descended slowly rather than plummeting. Steve, strapped precariously into the central harness, let out a delighted squawk of pure joy.

Then, the "directional stability" provided by the tree fungus failed. The glider veered sharply to the left, spun like a dizzy green top, and landed with a surprisingly soft thud directly into the lushest, most magnificent patch of mosses known to Kakapo-kind.

Steve emerged, covered head to toe in soft green moss, looking like a cheerful, fuzzy boulder. He shook himself, a shower of moss falling around him.

"Kevin!" he chirped, eyes wide with wonder. "We did it! We didn't fly, but we definitely descended with control! And look! The moss! It's the very best kind!"

Kevin, peering down from the ridge, a triumphant smile spreading across his beak, waddled down to join his friend. "Indeed, Steve. Indeed. Perhaps we haven't mastered the sky, but we have certainly mastered the art of targeted, controlled descent into optimal foraging locations. The Wright Brothers would be proud. Or utterly bewildered."

From that day on, Kevin and Steve became the unofficial "Airborne Access Specialists" of Whenua Hou. Their "glider" didn't truly fly, but it provided them with a rather efficient (and hilariously clumsy) way to get from high points directly into prime foraging spots, bypassing all the tedious waddling in between. They never fully achieved true flight, but they certainly had the most interesting commute in all of New Zealand, proving that even a flightless parrot can dream big, and perhaps, with enough determination (and a very understanding patch of moss), achieve a version of it.

THE SCENT OF LAVENDER AND CHAOS

Arthur Finch, a widower of seven years, viewed social gatherings with the same enthusiasm one might reserve for a root canal, without the promise of subsequent relief. His daughters Brenda, Jennifer, and Amanda were his support during the terrible time that followed his wife's passing.

His Ruth had had a relapse of cancer, and it really did a number on her. She peacefully passed away in his arms in the intensive care unit at the local hospital.

Over the next few years, the girls, all career-oriented women, did the best they could to encourage Arthur to live just like their mother would have wanted him.

Jennifer and her partner lived in Paris, where Jennifer was a fashion designer with a lot of work and little time for him. Meanwhile Amanda was in New York working for a large worldwide financial institution. She was divorced and travelling about eighty percent of her time, but never to Australia since that was not her territory.

That left Amanda, the youngest, and they stayed connected via Facetime from Hong Kong, where she was working for an IT company.

Amanda was a woman whose boundless optimism was matched only by her strategic use of guilt. With such gifts she had found and enrolled him in a local group—something called "Grief & Grin: Finding Your Spark After Loss."

Arthur privately suspected the "spark" in question was likely static electricity from cheap polyester, but Brenda had threatened to buy him a participation trophy if he didn't attend. And Arthur, a man who once argued with a pigeon over a discarded chip, would rather face a charging bull than a Brenda-induced lecture on "emotional processing."

The first meeting was in the Northport Community Hall, a place smelling faintly of existential dread. Arthur sat ramrod straight, a bastion of sartorial disapproval in his sensible tweed, observing the room. He saw various stages of grief: the perpetually teary, the aggressively cheerful, and the few, like himself, who merely looked as if they'd mistakenly wandered into a telethon for expressive feelings.

Then she arrived. Beatrice "Bea" Ponsonby.

She didn't just walk in, she bounced in, gloriously.

Her hair, a magnificent explosion of reddish curls, seemed to defy gravity and perhaps a few laws of physics. She wore a shocking fuchsia cardigan that threatened to blind Arthur and wore the tightest jeans he had ever seen on a woman. It accentuated her "assets" even more. Finally, her smile was so wide, and it looked so genuine it brought a big smile to his face. Adding to that, she looked to be in her late forties and was incredibly attractive.

She was everything Arthur wasn't vibrant.

Unreserved, outgoing, and apparently immune to the solemnity that bereavement was meant to inspire.

"Hello, everyone!" Bea chirped, her voice a delightful, slightly off-key bell. "Bea Ponsonby here! Lost my dear Bertram two years ago. Choked on a stubborn macaroon. Died happy, though, bless his sugary heart."

Arthur blinked.

Choked on a macaron?

His wife, bless her, had passed peacefully in his arms. He'd always considered that the gold standard of exits.

Macaron-related demise seemed untidy.

The group leader, a woman named Sharon who looked as if she'd swallowed a self-help manual whole, suggested a "light-hearted icebreaker."

Each person was to share a funny anecdote about their departed loved one. Arthur groaned internally. His life with Ruth had been many things. Comfortable, loving, quietly humorous, but a "light-hearted anecdote" wasn't exactly what sprang to mind when recalling her valiant, yet ultimately doomed, attempt to assemble IKEA furniture.

As the circle shrunk, Arthur braced himself.

"Arthur Finch," he announced when it was his turn, his voice a gravelly monotone. "My wife, Ruth, once, she accidentally put salt in the sugar bowl." He paused, awaiting the uproarious laughter that never came. A few polite nods. He mentally awarded himself a D- for effort.

Bea was next. "Oh, Bertram!" she exclaimed, a theatrical sigh escaping her lips. "He was a man of routines. Every Tuesday, he'd go to the library. One Tuesday, he forgot his trousers. Walked all the way there in his boxers, thinking they were shorts! The librarian called me. Said he was 'disturbing the peace' with his 'bare-legged literary pursuit'."

A ripple of genuine laughter, not just polite nods, swept through the room.

Arthur felt a flicker of something akin to annoyance.

Showing up trouser-less to a library was hardly a testament to one's wit. It was, rather, a testament to one's absent-mindedness. Yet, Bea told it with such flair, one might think Bertram had orchestrated the whole thing as a performance art piece.

Over the next few weeks, the "Grief & Grin" group morphed, for Arthur, into "Grief & Grimace," largely because of Bea's persistent presence.

Their tête-à-tête wasn't overtly hostile, but a subtle, ongoing contest of wills and worldviews.

If Arthur offered a cynical, dry observation, Bea would counter with a burst of effervescent optimism that felt, to him, almost aggressively cheerful.

During one session, Sharon introduced "expressive art therapy."

Arthur was handed a crayon and told to draw his feelings. He drew a stick figure sitting on a bench, looking bored. Bea, meanwhile, was creating a kaleidoscopic explosion of glitter, feathers, and what appeared to be a discarded tea bag, proclaiming it represented "Bertram's unbridled spirit, forever dancing amongst the cosmos."

"Looks like a craft project gone wrong at a particularly enthusiastic kindergarten," Arthur muttered under his breath, but Bea, with her preternatural hearing, snapped her head around.

"Oh, Mr Finch! And your profound masterpiece, a testament to the thrilling inner life of a garden gnome, I presume?" she retorted, a twinkle in her eye.

"Better a gnome than a glitter bomb," he grumbled, but he couldn't help but notice the corner of her mouth twitch.

Their encounters extended beyond the community hall.

Arthur, a creature of routines himself, frequented the same local bakery for his morning scone and coffee. One Tuesday, he walked in to find Bea, her fuchsia cardigan replaced by an equally blinding turquoise, haggling with the baker over the correct shade of sprinkles for a cake.

"Arthur! Fancy meeting you here!" she trilled, as if their shared postcode wasn't the most obvious explanation. "Just arranging Bertram's annual 'Macaroon Memorial Celebration.' He adored macaroons, even though it was his undoing."

Arthur just nodded, trying to avoid eye contact with Bea and just said aloud to the server: "My scone, please and a latte."

"Right. A scone and a latte. Coming right up."

"Still stuck on the scone, Arthur?" she questioned, a mock-sympathetic pout on her lips. "Live a little! Try a croissant! Or a pain au chocolat! The pastry of adventure!"

"Adventure, Mrs Ponsonby, is getting the heating bill down in winter. Not a bread product," Arthur countered, paying for his scone with a brisk finality.

Bea merely laughed, a sound that made the display case vibrate. "You're a real firecracker, aren't you, Arthur? A very, very damp firecracker."

The ultimate arena for their ongoing, unspoken rivalry presented itself in the form of the group's annual charity bake sale. Sharon, with her usual unshakeable cheer, announced it as an opportunity to "spread joy through confectionery."

Arthur, whose culinary skills began and ended with boiling water, felt a cold dread.

Sharon immediately volunteered. "My David makes a mean—well, made—he was very good at opening biscuit packets!" she'd chirped.

Bea, naturally, was already envisioning a confectionery empire. "I'm making my famous 'Bertram's Blissful

Brownies.' They're so fudgy, they almost melt into the space-time continuum!" she boasted during the next meeting.

Arthur, cornered, declared, "I'll be making my special lemon drizzle cake." He had, in fact, never made a lemon drizzle cake. His only experience with lemons involved slicing them for gin and tonics.

The day of the bake sale dawned bright and terrifyingly sunny. Bea's table was a riot of colour and sugar. Her "Blissful Brownies" were indeed fudgy, glistening with a suspiciously professional-looking ganache. She also had "Bertram's Boisterous Baklava" and "Ponsonby's Peculiar Pumpkin Pies."

Arthur's table looked like a crime scene involving a flour bag and a very confused citrus fruit. His "special lemon drizzle cake" was less drizzle, more concrete slab, and decidedly un lemon-like in both colour and texture. It had a faint greenish tinge that he blamed on the fluorescent lights. He'd tried to follow a recipe but had clearly misread "cup" for "bucket" when it came to the flour.

"Arthur, darling! Your cake!" Bea exclaimed, strolling over, a smug glint in her eye. "It has character. And a certain density. Is that a new architectural style?"

"It's rustic, Bea. Unlike your confections, which look like a team of highly paid sugar elves sculpted them," Arthur retorted, adjusting a price tag that had fallen off his cake.

"Oh, they are!" Bea declared, completely missing the sarcasm. "I have remarkably high standards. And Bertram would have wanted nothing less for his legacy." She then added in a stage whisper, "Though I think he might have used yours as a doorstop."

The bake sale progressed, Bea's table doing a roaring trade. People approached Arthur's cake with a mixture of curiosity and apprehension, eventually settling for buying one of Brenda's store-bought cookies she discreetly placed at the back.

Suddenly, a small child, drawn by the faint promise of sugar, pointed at Arthur's cake. "Mummy, is that a rock?"

Bea burst into laughter, a loud, uninhibited sound that made Arthur's ears burn. "No, sweetie," she said, wiping a tear from her eye. "That's Mr Finch's 'concrete couture' cake."

Arthur, surprisingly, found himself not entirely annoyed. Her laughter, for all its boisterousness, was infectious. And the child was right; it looked like a rock.

Later, as the bake sale wound down, Arthur sat slumped in a folding chair, counting the measly proceeds from his non cake. Bea, surprisingly, joined him, carrying two cups of coffee.

"So, 'concrete couture,' eh?" he said, a faint smile playing on his lips.

"Well, admit, it was a bold choice," Bea replied, taking a sip. "Though I saw one gentleman attempt to cut it with a butter knife and then give up and gnaw on it like a beaver."

Arthur chuckled; a dry, rusty sound he rarely emitted. "It had a good chew."

"It certainly did," Bea agreed, then her voice softened slightly. "You know, Arthur, for a man who claims to hate socialising, you've been rather… entertaining."

He looked at her, really looked at her, for the first time without the lens of his self-imposed grumpiness. Her eyes, though framed by laughter lines, held a kindness he hadn't noticed.

"And you, Mrs Ponsonby," he began, surprising himself. "For a woman who uses more glitter than a Las Vegas showgirl, you're not entirely insufferable."

She threw her head back and laughed again. "High praise indeed, Mr Finch! I shall engrave that on Bertram's macaron memorial."

The silence that followed wasn't awkward, but surprisingly comfortable. Then Bea spoke, almost hesitantly. "Sharon's organising a small group outing next week. A visit to the botanical gardens. Nothing too strenuous. Lots of benches to sit on if one gets architecturally fatigued."

Arthur considered it.

Botanical gardens.

Greenery.

Relative quiet.

And Bea.

He could imagine her pointing out every single flower with an exclamation mark attached. He could also imagine himself making a pithy comment about the invasive species of her enthusiasm.

"Are they serving coffee there?" he asked, a twinkle in his own eye.

Bea grinned. "I believe there's a rather charming little café. They do a decent coffee and scone, I'm told. Though perhaps not as robust as your culinary creations."

Arthur pushed himself up from the chair. "Fine. But if you try to make me hug a tree, I'm calling Brenda."

Bea merely laughed, a sound like sunshine after a long grey spell. "Deal, Arthur. Deal."

As they walked towards the exit, their shoulders brushed. A small, accidental contact.

The tête-à-tête wasn't over, not by a long shot. But the sting had gone out of the sparring, replaced by a warmth that felt, surprisingly, rather pleasant.

Arthur realised, with a jolt, that he hadn't thought about static electricity all afternoon.

A few months ambled by, turning the gentle friction between Arthur and Bea into something less like sandpaper and more like a well-oiled hinge. Their "tête-à-tête" had evolved. It began subtly, with late-night phone calls that started as debriefs on Sharon's latest "emotional mosaic" session and ended with Arthur offering surprisingly nuanced criticisms of Bea's daring fashion choices, and Bea retorting with equally precise observations about the increasing eccentricity of Arthur's knitwear.

Then came the accidental late-night visit.

Arthur, suffering from a bout of insomnia brought on by an overly dramatic true-crime documentary, found himself inexplicably outside Bea's brightly painted front door at 2 AM. Bea, equally insomniac and in the middle of attempting to re tile her bathroom while wearing a silk dressing gown had answered the door without thinking.

A shared, awkward laugh, a cup of chamomile tea, and a surprising confession from Arthur that he was rather lonely, led to, well, one thing led to another. And then to another. And then to a discreet, but undeniably regular, arrangement.

Their "friends with benefits" situation was, in typical Arthur and Bea fashion, less a passionate whirlwind and more a series of highly practical, mildly chaotic encounters. There were no declarations of undying affection, merely mutually agreed-upon terms: "No glitter in the bedroom, Bea," Arthur had laid down, sternly. "And Arthur, darling, if you snore, I reserve the right to gently prod you with a decorative cushion," Bea had countered, reasonably.

The benefits were varied.

For Arthur, it was the unexpected warmth, the comfort of another presence in the otherwise quiet house, and the sheer comedic value of Bea's morning hair. For Bea, it was the surprising steadiness of Arthur's presence, his quiet, dry wit, and that he was surprisingly good at fixing leaky taps while she was otherwise occupied.

Their mornings after were often a study in comedic contrasts. Arthur, ever the traditionalist, would be quietly making coffee while Bea, still in her silk dressing gown, would be enthusiastically planning breakfast, usually involving something alarmingly colourful and sticky.

"Morning, Arthur! I'm thinking blueberry pancakes with a side of 'Bertram's Boisterous Bacon'—he always said bacon should be crispy enough to shatter dreams!" she'd announce, waving a spatula perilously close to his head.

Arthur would sigh contentedly into his teacup. "Just the coffee, Bea. And perhaps less boisterous bacon this morning. My dreams are quite fragile."

Brenda, of course, was oblivious.

She still called regularly, inquiring about his "spark" and suggesting new, equally dreadful, social groups. "How's 'Grief & Grin,' Dad? Still finding your feet?"

"Oh, I'm finding my feet, Brenda," Arthur would reply, glancing at Bea, who was currently attempting to juggle three oranges while humming an operatic aria. "And other things. Quite well, actually."

Bea would wink, and Arthur would pretend to clear his throat, a faint blush creeping up his neck. Their arrangement wasn't about romance in the conventional sense, not yet anyway. It was about companionship, shared laughter, and the peculiar comfort of two vastly different people finding a perfectly imperfect rhythm.

It was, Arthur conceded, far less painful than a root canal, and significantly more amusing. And sometimes, after Bea had left, leaving behind a faint scent of vanilla and chaos, Arthur would smile—a genuine, unforced smile. He even caught himself humming a slightly off-key tune once, a habit he hadn't had since Ruth.

The "spark," it seemed, had finally arrived, in the most unlikely and un-polyester-like of forms.

One evening, as the last vestiges of twilight clung to the sky and the scent of Bea's overly enthusiastic aromatherapy diffuser filled Arthur's living room, Arthur cleared his throat.

"Bea," he began, surprising himself with the sudden earnestness in his voice. He paused, collecting his thoughts, which felt like herding particularly stubborn cats. "This arrangement. Your companionship, your laughter, even your glitter-adjacent clothing. And, well, our intimacy in bed." He hesitated, fumbling for the right words. "I value it. Immensely. But I-I can't bring myself to say I love you."

Bea, who had been meticulously polishing a ceramic frog, looked up, her expression surprisingly soft, devoid of its usual effervescence.

"Oh, Arthur, darling."

She put the frog down with a gentle clink.

"Did you really think I expected you to?"

She reached across the worn armchair and gently patted his hand.

"My heart, like yours, gave its profound, unshakeable love to my Bertram. And yours to your Ruth. That kind of love, Arthur, it's not something you just recycle."

A small, almost imperceptible sadness flickered in her eyes, quickly replaced by her usual resilient twinkle. "But what we have, this peculiar dance of ours? It's special. Unique. It fills a different kind of space, doesn't it?"

Arthur nodded, a sense of immense relief washing over him. "It does."

"So," Bea continued, her voice gaining a touch of its usual briskness, "if you wish, we can remain exclusive. Demand nothing more of each other than this delightful silliness and the occasional shared insomnia. No pressure, no awkward declarations, just us. And our rules about glitter."

Arthur's lips curved into a genuine, if slight, smile. "I wish."

Bea's face broke into a wide, triumphant grin. "Wonderful! Now, let's make whoopee like the Yanks say, before one of us kicks the bucket!"

Arthur chuckled, a warm, resonant sound.

He simply took Bea's hand, his fingers intertwining with hers, and led her towards the bedroom, the scent of lavender and chaos trailing behind them.

THE STEERING WHEEL INCIDENT

Anna Smith, a woman whose retirement from public school teaching had gifted her an abundance of time and a renewed interest in the peculiar dance of modern romance, sat across from her best friend, Allison Mallory, at their usual haunt, "The Northport Café and Bakery." The aroma of coffee and existential dread hung heavy in the air, a comforting backdrop to their weekly gossip sessions.

"Honestly, Allison," Anna sighed, stirring her lukewarm latte, "it's like they've all been replaced by pod people. Every man I meet either talks only about his cryptocurrency portfolio or asks if I've seen his missing sock."

Allison, a whirlwind of vibrant scarves and even more vibrant opinions, snorted into her latte. "Darling, you're looking in the wrong cryptos. You need a man with pizzazz. Someone who can quote Rilke in three languages and still knows how to fix a leaky faucet."

"A unicorn, then," Anna deadpanned, but a flicker of hope danced in her eyes. She secretly yearned for intellectual stimulation, a partner who could navigate a conversation beyond the weather and the price of gas.

It was precisely then, as if summoned by Allison's dramatic pronouncement, that he appeared. He did not exactly appear so much as he glided into their peripheral vision, a smooth, dark-haired man with eyes that seemed to hold the secrets of ancient civilisations and a smile that promised exotic adventures. He was, to Anna's surprise, speaking to Allison, who had apparently excused herself to fetch more sugar and had, in typical Allison fashion, struck up a conversation with a complete stranger.

Anna watched, fascinated, as Allison gestured wildly, her usual conversational style, while the man leaned in, his voice a low, melodic murmur. He laughed, a rich, genuine sound, and then, to Anna's astonishment, he seamlessly transitioned from English to what sounded suspiciously like French, then a smattering of Italian, and finally, a few rapid-fire sentences in what Anna suspected was Mandarin, all in response to Allison's increasingly bewildered expressions.

When Allison finally returned, her eyes wide with a mixture of awe and confusion, she practically collapsed into her chair. "Anna, you will not believe this man. He's like a walking Rosetta Stone! He just asked me if I prefer my sugar 'cubed, granulated, or in the sweet whisper of a forgotten dialect."

Anna, ever the pragmatist, raised an eyebrow. "And what did you say?"

"I panicked and said 'yes, please!" Allison wailed. "But he's absolutely charming, and he kept looking over here, at you."

And indeed, he was.

He was now making his way towards their table, a confident, easy stride that bespoke a man comfortable in his own skin, and probably in several time zones.

"Anna Smith, may I introduce you to Dr. Alistair Finch," Allison announced, beaming like a proud matchmaker. "He's a linguist! And he said he'd love to buy us another round of whatever this delightful concoction is."

Alistair Finch.

Even his name sounded like a poet had handcrafted it.

He bowed slightly, a gesture so unexpectedly old-world charming that Anna almost spilled her chamomile. He spoke to her then, his voice a warm baritone, effortlessly weaving between topics, quoting obscure poets, discussing geopolitical nuances, and even offering a surprisingly insightful critique of the cafe's questionable jazz music, all while maintaining impeccable eye contact. He even made a joke about the missing sock phenomenon, and Anna laughed, a genuine, unforced laugh that hadn't escaped her lips in years.

He was everything Anna had subtly, secretly, and perhaps a little desperately, wished for.

He was intelligent, witty, worldly, and possessed a smile that could melt glaciers.

When he asked her out for dinner that very evening, Anna, usually cautious, agreed with an uncharacteristic alacrity.

The dinner was, predictably, delightful.

Alistair was an attentive conversationalist, a connoisseur of fine wines, and, surprisingly, a fantastic storyteller. He recounted tales of his travels, his linguistic adventures, and even a humorous anecdote about mistaking a goat for an aggressive garden gnome in rural Tuscany. Anna felt a lightness she hadn't experienced in years, a genuine connection that transcended the usual awkward first-date pleasantries.

It was on the drive home, the city lights blurring into streaks of colour, that the first tremor of unease began.

Alistair was navigating the winding suburban streets with practiced ease; his hands relaxed on the steering wheel.

Anna was mid-sentence, describing her particularly challenging third-grade class and their penchant for glitter-bombing everything, when she noticed it.

He released his left hand from the wheel, just for a fraction of a second, and brought it swiftly to his mouth. A quick, almost imperceptible lick. Then his hand was back on the wheel, as if nothing had happened.

Anna paused, mid-glitter-bomb.

Did I just see that? She wondered.

She dismissed it.

Perhaps he had a crumb on his finger.

A stray piece of lint.

A momentary itch.

She resumed her story, but a tiny, insistent voice in the back of her mind had been awakened.

A few minutes later, as he smoothly rounded a corner, he did it again.

This time, it was his right hand.

A quick release, a swift lick, a return to the wheel.

It was so fast, so fluid, it almost seemed like part of his natural driving rhythm.

Anna's internal monologue went into overdrive.

Is he tasting the steering wheel?

Is there a secret flavour?

Is it a nervous tic?

Does he have dry hands?

But why just the palms?

And why so secretively?

The charm, which had previously enveloped her like a warm blanket, now felt like a slightly too-tight straitjacket.

Every few minutes, like a macabre metronome, the hand would lift, the tongue would dart, and the hand would return.

Anna found herself mesmerised, watching his hands more than listening to his fascinating discourse on the etymology of the word "serendipity."

By the time he pulled up to her curb, a growing sense of bewildered horror had replaced the enchantment. He walked her to the door, his smile still dazzling, his farewell in flawless, lyrical Portuguese. Anna managed a polite thank you, her mind still replaying the bizarre hand-licking ballet.

The moment the door clicked shut, she grabbed her phone and dialled Allison. It rang once, twice, then Allison's breathless voice answered.

"Well? Details! Was he everything I said he was? Did he quote more Rilke? Did you swoon?"

"Allison," Anna began, her voice a low, conspiratorial whisper, "he was perfect. Charming, intelligent, spoke seven languages, probably eight if you count the language of love."

"I knew it!" Allison shrieked. "I told you, Anna, you just needed a man with…"

"But then," Anna interrupted, her voice dropping even lower, "on the drive home now and then, he'd release the steering wheel and quickly lick his hands."

Silence stretched across the line, punctuated only by Allison's sharp intake of breath. Then, a dramatic gasp.

"Oh, no," Allison whispered, her voice laced with a horror usually reserved for discovering a spider in her artisanal cheese. "Oh, no. It's the 'ick."

"The what now?" Anna asked, though a part of her instinctively understood.

"The 'ick'!"

Allison practically screamed, the word echoing with the weight of a thousand failed romances.

"That sudden pang of aversion, usually prompted by someone's behaviour, appearance, or personality trait! It's like your brain just slams the emergency brakes on any burgeoning attraction! The steering wheel licking! Anna, that's a five-star, platinum-level 'ick'!"

Anna chewed on her lip. "But why? Why would he do that? Was he tasting the leather? Is it some obscure cultural habit I'm unaware of? Is he a secret lizard person?"

"It doesn't matter why, Anna!" Allison wailed. "The 'ick' is not rational! It just is! It's the universe telling you, 'Nope! Not this one! He licks steering wheels!"

"But he's so charming!" Anna protested weakly, picturing Alistair's dazzling smile, now tainted by the image of a darting tongue.

"Charm doesn't override the 'ick,' Anna. The 'ick' is a force of nature," Allison declared with the solemnity of a seasoned anthropologist. "It's like trying to put out a bonfire with a single tear. Once the 'ick' sets in, it's a permanent resident. You'll never unsee the steering wheel licking. You'll be on a romantic gondola ride in Venice, and all you'll be able to think about is him licking the oar."

Anna shuddered. The thought of Alistair, the multilingual charmer, licking a gondola oar, was indeed a powerful deterrent. The image was now irrevocably linked.

"So, what do I do?" Anna asked, feeling a strange mix of disappointment and morbid fascination.

"You thank him for the lovely evening. Tell him you're suddenly allergic to polyurethane, and then you run,"

Allison advised, her voice firm. "You run like the wind, Anna. Before the 'ick' spreads to other objects. Before he starts licking the saltshaker. Or, heaven forbid, your hand."

Anna hung up, a small, rueful smile playing on her lips.

She had found her unicorn, a man of intellect and charm, who could converse in a symphony of languages. But alas, her unicorn also had a peculiar, deeply unsettling habit.

The "ick" had arrived, swift and decisive, like a well aimed glitter bomb.

And Anna, a retired public-school teacher, knew better than anyone that once the glitter was out, it was impossible to get rid of.

COST OF IMPATIENCE

A hurried world, a ticking clock,

Each app demands, a second's shock.

Employers push for gains right now,

Investments lure, "Trade, take a bow!"

But while the market churns and screams,

A quiet hand fulfills its dreams.

The patient soul, who held the line,

Now owns the street, a slow design.

For hasty hands will often lose,

What steady, waiting hands diffuse.

The patient win, the long game's prize,

Inheriting what haste denies.

SUSANNAH'S BIG BREAK

Larry's potato brow furrowed as fellow potato Walter shared the news of Susannah's selection.

"Larry, Larry, did you hear?" Walter's voice, usually a booming rumble, was hushed, almost reverent.

"What, Walter?" Larry responded, his attention caught by the unusual solemnity in his friend's tone.

"Susannah was finally picked. She is going to be processed this week and will leave our little community."

A slow, knowing smile spread across Larry's face. "How wonderful, Walter. How does she feel about being chosen?"

"Just great. She always thought she was plump enough to be chosen, but every year, year after year, those damn American Idaho potatoes were picked over her." Walter's voice held a lingering hint of bitterness, a shared grievance among the Australian spuds.

"Well, Walter, I am so glad that an Aussie spud will now be the reigning queen of this year's packaging contest." Larry puffed out his chest a little, a flicker of national pride igniting in his starchy core.

"True, so true, Walter, but does Susannah understand or know the entire process? Have you told her?" Larry's question hung in the air, weighted with unspoken concerns.

Walter shifted uncomfortably, a fine layer of dust dislodging from his skin. "No, Larry, and don't you dare tell her. All she needs to know is that she will be on the cover of the packaging bag, and she will be famous."

Larry's gaze drifted beyond their immediate patch, towards the distant hum of the "Processing Plant," a looming structure that cast a long shadow over Spudville. He had seen others go, plump and proud, never to return. The "fame" Walter spoke of was a bittersweet currency.

"Yes, yes, of course," Larry conceded, though his voice lacked conviction. "How long will this fame and notoriety last, Walter? Do you know?"

Walter's usual bluster seemed to deflate. He looked at Larry, his round, brown eyes reflecting a deep, ancient sadness. "Until the last bite, Larry. Just until the last bite."

A silence settled between them, broken only by the gentle rustle of leaves as a breeze swept through the field.

Susannah, in her youthful exuberance, was already preening, imagining her glossy image adorning supermarket shelves. She dreamed of being admired, of being the star of countless family dinners. She didn't dream of the peeler, the slicer, the hot oil, or the hungry mouths.

And for now, Larry knew, it was better that way.

Their job, as the silent guardians of Spudville, was to let her shine, however briefly, in the fleeting spotlight of her destined glory.

WHOSE FAULT WAS IT

In the fluorescent-lit belly of Consolidated United Bank (CUB, for short, and fitting, because employees often felt trapped in a confined space), the 14th floor buzzed with mild anxiety and the scent of old coffee. It was Thursday, otherwise known in the Customer Solutions Department as "Crisis Planning Day," where issues were "addressed" in meetings and never fully solved.

At 9:02 AM, Manager Ted Brubaker barged into the glass-walled conference room with the urgency of a man who had just discovered the copier was jammed with someone's tuna melt.

"Elizabeth!" he barked, startling the only other person in the room: Elizabeth Montoya, the Supervisor of Customer Service and reigning champion of passive aggressive email tone.

She sipped her coffee calmly. "Good morning, Ted. I see the caffeine's working."

"We're twenty-seven percent over budget!" Ted exclaimed, dropping a folder full of colourful pie charts and bar graphs onto the table like they were tarot cards of doom.

Elizabeth blinked. "Is that so? What happened? Did our call centre agents unionise and start demanding more healthcare and decent lighting?"

Ted paced. "No, no, nothing like that. It's the coffee subscription, the pizza Fridays, the emotional support chinchilla initiative."

"First," Elizabeth interrupted, holding up a hand, "Paco, the Chinchilla, has saved lives. There hasn't been a breakdown in the break room since he arrived."

"He's very fluffy, I'll give you that," Ted mumbled. Then, more loudly: "But we need to make cuts. Drastic cuts."

Elizabeth raised an eyebrow. "Define 'drastic.'"

"We may need to consider layoffs."

A silence descended upon the conference room, broken only by the distant hum of someone aggressively typing their way through a customer complaint about their overdraft fee being rounded up.

Elizabeth leaned back in her chair. "Layoffs, huh? So, we're solving a budgeting problem by removing the people who solve problems."

Ted blinked. "It's a simple equation. Fewer people equal a smaller payroll. Less payroll equals happier finance guys. Happier finance guys equal fewer middle-of-the-night text messages asking why we spent $78 on foam stress bananas."

"That was for our 'De-Stress Your Desk' initiative. It worked until Troy from Accounts started eating them."

Ted slapped the folder again. "Elizabeth, we're spiralling. I need solutions. I need ideas. I need sacrifices!"

Elizabeth set her mug down carefully, as if she were about to say something illegal.

"Okay, fine. Let's brainstorm," she said sweetly. "We could switch our coffee supplier to that off-brand one that tastes like regret and carpet fuzz."

"Already did," Ted said grimly. "HR revolted. One of them tried to unionise with the janitorial staff and the AI chatbot."

"Hmm. Then what about automating part of our team's work? Replace the chat agents with a bot."

"We tried that last quarter. The bot started recommending customers apply for bankruptcy. And one time it just typed 'vibes' when asked about interest rates."

"Bold of it," Elizabeth muttered. "What if we cut team birthdays? No more cupcakes."

"Julie from customer service has threatened legal action if we touch her Funfetti Fridays."

Elizabeth sighed. "Fine. Then what if we switch to a hybrid work model?"

Ted shook his head. "Already tried it. Half the staff just disappeared into the abyss. Said they were working from 'deep focus caves' in national parks."

Elizabeth tapped a pen against her notebook. "Alright, alright. So, layoffs it is unless…"

Ted's ears perked up. "Unless?"

Elizabeth leaned forward. Her tone grew thoughtful, like a detective about to explain the twist in a murder mystery.

"Let's look at this logically. Who made the budget?"

Ted hesitated. "I did."

"And who said we were on track, despite me mentioning multiple times that we were spending too much on inflatable furniture for the break room?"

"That was also me."

"And who, just last month, allocated $3,000 for what was labelled 'strategic morale experiences' that turned out to be an escape room where you cried in the coat closet?"

Ted pointed a finger. "Hey! That was team bonding!"

"You shouted, 'I should have become a vet!' while sobbing into a fake spiderweb."

Ted's finger lowered. "Okay, fine. It wasn't my best budgeting moment."

Elizabeth gave a slow, graceful shrug. "So then, maybe the person who did the budget and didn't stick to the budget is the one who should be laid off."

Ted's jaw dropped. "You want to fire me?"

She smiled serenely. "Just thinking aloud. It's not personal, Ted. It's budgetary. You said we needed sacrifices."

"But, but I'm the manager!"

"Exactly. A noble sacrifice." She paused dramatically. "Think about the headlines: 'Manager Accepts Blame for Budgetary Blunders, Saves Dozens of Jobs and Chinchilla.' You'd be a hero."

Ted looked stunned. "You're actually serious."

"Oh no," Elizabeth replied, sipping her coffee again. "I'm completely unserious. It's just a fun little idea. Like putting beanbags in the conference room or trusting you with the corporate card."

There was a long pause. Ted stared at the wall, re evaluating every career decision since he'd skipped accounting school to get an MBA with a minor in 'Visioneering.'

Then he shook his head. "Nope. Not happening. I can't fire myself."

Elizabeth raised an eyebrow. "Okay. Then what about promoting me above you so I can fire you?"

"Elizabeth!"

"I'm just spit balling here. You asked for ideas."

Ted flopped into a chair and buried his face in his hands. "You're evil."

She nodded. "And fiscally responsible."

After a long silence, Ted peeked through his fingers. "Okay, fine. We're not firing me. But maybe we look at cutting that internal podcast no one listens to."

"Oh, 'Finance & Feelings'? Yeah, no one needs to hear Carl from legal cry about tax season again."

Ted sighed. "And the nap pods."

Elizabeth gasped. "Not the nap pods!"

"I'm sorry, but we're desperate."

They sat in silence, both mourning the future of lunch-hour naps, before Elizabeth spoke up again.

"What if," she said, "we cut back on spending, keep everyone employed and make you take a budgeting refresher course? Maybe from someone qualified. Like a fifth grader who runs a lemonade stand."

Ted glared. "You're very smug for someone who wears pyjamas on Casual Friday."

"They're technically lounge slacks," she said primly. "But sure. I'll take a smug. Because I just saved your department."

Ted sighed. "Fine. No layoffs. No firing me. But we are taking Paco the Chinchilla off the payroll."

Elizabeth narrowed her eyes. "Say that again, and he'll chew through your shoelaces while you sleep."

Ted got up slowly. "You're terrifying."

She nodded. "And budget friendly."

Two Weeks Later

The department remained intact.

The coffee was worse, the nap pods were replaced with beanbags filled with packing peanuts, and the budget now had a section labelled "Ask Elizabeth Before Buying Weird Stuff."

Ted completed his budgeting course and began referring to himself as "Finance Minded Ted," which didn't catch on.

Paco the Chinchilla was promoted to "Chief Emotional Officer," and HR requested he be cloned.

And Elizabeth?

Elizabeth got a raise.

Because sometimes, the best budget fix is just knowing whose fault it was in the first place.

THE SPA AND RESORT

Let me introduce myself.

I'm Abbie. Not Abigail, not Abster, not "who's a good girl?" (though the answer is obviously me).

Just Abbie. I'm a seven-year-old, bitsa dog. A bit of Australian kettle dog and a bit some sort of terrier (my mum never told me). I have and live a good life with my human, Andrea, and her mother, Elizabeth. They love me, feed me, talk to me like I'm the baby in their house. They even let me sleep at the foot of their bed unless I'm being "wiggly." Whatever that means.

Now, don't get me wrong, home is pleasant.

But there is a magical place, a canine paradise where the grass is greener, the treats flow like bacon waterfalls, and no one ever says, "Stop it."

This place?

My owner's grandparent's house, otherwise known as the Grandpawrent Resort and Spa.

Whenever I hear the words "We're going on a cruise and you have to stay with Mum and Papi-Hose," I do a full-body wag that starts at my nose and ends with my tail breaking the sound barrier. I don't even wait for either of them to put on my leash. I'm already in the car, sitting in the back seat like, "Let's go, woman! I've got naps to take and snacks to eat!"

The second we arrive, I know I'm home.

Not home home, but a better home. The kind with fluffier cushions and fewer rules.

The door bursts open, and there she is, Nanna. She squeals like she's just seen a celebrity, which, to be fair, she has.

"ABBIEEEEEE! My sweet little sugar paw pumpkin wiggle butt!"

I immediately collapse into a dramatic flop on the floor, exposing my belly like the shameless queen I am. She rubs it with both hands and coos like she's got a grandbaby and a minor wine buzz. "You must be exhausted from that long drive! Let's get you a snack!"

Snack? Sing it, Nanna. Sing the song of my people.

While Elizabeth is helping her mother bring in my stuff from the car, I'm already in the kitchen, sitting pretty like a canine ballet dancer. Nanna opens a magical cabinet, THE TREAT CABINET (they call it the fridge for some reason), and out comes a treat of some sort.

She pulls out a "chewy filet-wrapped duck sweet potato twist," which, I swear, is fancier than anything Elizabeth eats.

One twist?

Ha.

I get three.

Because Nanna doesn't believe in limits.

Or portion control.

Papi-Hose appears next, coming out of the office.

He's not a squealer like Nanna, but he calls me "Miss Princess" and slips me many pats under the table like he's in a secret dog-treat mafia. One time during the Christmas lunch, he gave me an entire slice of turkey and whispered, "Don't tell your mum."

If I could respond to him, I would have said: "Sir, I would take this secret to the grave."

The couch?

I'm allowed on it, as long as the old sheet is spread on it.

It is time for bedtime.

The bed?

All mine.

Nanna and Papi-Hose tried to break me of this habit, but I won in the end.

I always win.

The next morning, the pampering continues. Nanna wakes me up gently.

"Abbie, sweetie, wanna go for a walk?"

She says "walk" like it's a holy pilgrimage.

And I'm ready.

I prance to the front door, waiting for my harness to be placed around my body, and I jump like I am a furry Olympic athlete.

I walk through the neighbourhood like I own it.

I pee on every blade of grass I smell, every mailbox that attracts me and the tyre of any car that looks at me sideways. Nanna brings a special pouch of liver treats and hands them over every time I glance back at her like, "You proud of me?" I think to myself.

I just peed on that Prius.

She is.

She's SO proud.

We pass other dogs who are clearly not staying at a five-star resort like me. They bark, desperate for attention. I don't bark back. I give them a look that says.

Peasant.

After the walk, I get a big pat. Not a quick single pat. No, I get a full-on service, five long, luscious pats.

Then comes breakfast time.

While Elizabeth believes in "dog food," the grandpawrents believe in "a little something special." Today it's leftover rice with a splash of chicken broth and a dollop of pumpkin. I eat like I'm at a Michelin-star restaurant for dogs.

Afternoons are for cuddles and watching Nanna's newest heartthrob Rob Lowe in '911 Lone Star'. I curl up next to Nanna, who snacks on crackers and cheese, and occasionally drops one "by accident." (This woman hasn't had a real accident in all the years I've been coming to her home).

Papi-Hose is busy in the office 'writing' his stories. I hope he never writes one about me.

One time, right when I was dropped off, I heard my owner Elizabeth say: "Mum, I think you are spoiling Abbie too much."

"Excuse me?"

Nanna said, "Oh, Elizabeth. She is our guest! And she's such a good girl!"

Did you hear that? Good girl. Boom. Case closed.

But my reign hit a slight bump the next day. Nanna was cleaning the back porch, tidying up, while I was doing my usual patrol of the backyard, peeing on imaginary threats, sniffing for intruder activity when I saw it.

A magpie.

A glorious, fast-as-lightning magpie.

Now, normally I'm all about lounging, but I am, at my core, a professional bird-chaser and part-time behind the window barker.

So, I took off like a missile.

"ABBIE!" Nanna yelled.

But the magpie was RIGHT THERE. I channelled my inner greyhound. I ran like the wind. I almost achieved liftoff.

Unfortunately, I also achieved something else—mud. Wet, sticky, freshly sprinkled mud. I hit it like a cartoon character and went splat, belly first, straight through the flowerbed, emerging on the other side like a chocolate-dipped hot dog.

Nanna stared at me.

I stared at Nanna.

Then, I gave her my best "I regret nothing" face and wagged my tail so hard it slung mud onto her garden clothes.

That night, I got a bath.

Now listen.

I don't like baths.

But this one?

Nanna went all the way out of her way.

A bubble bath.

Lavender-scented shampoo.

Warm water.

A blow-dryer with a diffuser.

It was a doggy spa, and I felt like I was Beyoncé.

After I was dry and smelling like a lilac candle, Nanna wrapped me in a towel and said, "You're just too cute to stay mad at."

I know, Nanna. I know.

When it was finally time to go home, I pulled out every trick in the book.

Sad eyes.

Dramatic sighs.

Sitting by the front door like, No, I live here now. I even carried my favourite stuffed duck to Nanna's feet and made a soft "mrrrph" noise, which is universally understood to mean "don't make me go back to the peasants."

Andrea, the traitor, picked up my leash anyway.

"Say goodbye, Abbie."

Nanna sniffled. "You'll come back soon, won't you?"

Oh, I will. I'll be back. And I expect the filet-wrapped sweet potato twists to be waiting.

Back home, things returned to normal. Fewer treats. No recliner cuddles. A distinct lack of turkey slices.

But sometimes when I'm lying on the couch (not technically allowed, but I do it anyway), I dream of the Grandpawrent Resort.

And in those dreams, I'm wearing a tiny robe, holding a squeaky toy mimosa, while Nanna whispers, "Who's ready for her massage?"

It's me, Nanna. It's always me.

MINIMUM WAGE

Barry, a man whose relentless squeak rivalled whose perpetual state of optimism only in his Corolla's suspension, hummed a jaunty tune as he navigated the labyrinthine streets of inner-city Sydney.

July 1st, 2025.

A date etched on his calendar, not for a birthday or an anniversary, but for something far more significant: the glorious, life-altering, potentially toastie-with-two-cheeses-on-it minimum wage increase in Australia.

"It's a game-changer, Sheila!" he'd declared to his bewildered neighbour, Sheila, who was merely trying to retrieve her recycling bin. "No more scraping by! We're talking proper living wages now! Think of the possibilities!"

Sheila had just nodded; her eyes fixed on a rogue banana peel near Barry's tyre. Barry, however, was already mentally redecorating his modest apartment with an imaginary throw pillow that wasn't from Kmart.

For weeks, the news had been a balm to Barry's soul.

The Fair Work Commission, in its infinite wisdom, had decreed that the lowest earners in the land would receive a bump. Barry, a proud, if slightly perplexed, purveyor of Uber Eats, saw himself squarely in that demographic.

He envisioned a world where every chicken Katsu curry delivered, every lukewarm latte ferried, would contribute to a grander, more financially robust future. He'd even started practicing a more confident "Enjoy your meal!" in the mirror.

He figured a confident delivery person deserved a confident wage.

The morning of July 1st dawned.

He'd laid out his cleanest (least stained) Uber Eats jacket, polished his phone screen until it gleamed, and even gave his Corolla, affectionately named 'The Chariot of Culinary Delights,' a quick wipe-down.

This was it.

The day his financial woes evaporated like steam from a freshly delivered pho.

He logged onto the Uber Eats app, his thumb hovering over the "Go Online" button.

He expected fireworks.

A fanfare.

Perhaps a little animated confetti falling across the screen, accompanied by a notification: "Congratulations, Barry! Your new, magnificent hourly rate is now…!"

Instead, the app looked exactly the same.

The familiar map, the little car icon, the tantalising "Online" button.

No fanfare.

No confetti.

Not even a polite little pop-up saying, "G'day, Barry! Feeling richer yet?"

Barry frowned.

"Perhaps it's a backend update," he mused, tapping the screen vigorously. "They're probably rolling it out slowly, building the suspense."

His first order pinged: a single sausage roll from the bakery, 1.2 km away. The pay: $4.50. Barry blinked. $4.50.

That was exactly what it was yesterday.

And the day before.

And the month before.

"Hmm," he muttered, picking up the sausage roll.

"Maybe it's a per-hour thing. They'll tally it up at the end of the day and surprise me with a bonus!"

He pictured a little digital pot of gold overflowing with crisp Australian dollars.

He spent the next few hours ferrying various culinary delights across the city. Burgers, sushi, a suspiciously large order of kale smoothies. With each delivery, the same familiar, slightly underwhelming payout. By lunchtime, a tiny seed of doubt, no bigger than a sesame seed on a burger bun, sprouted in Barry's optimistic mind.

He pulled over for a quick break, parking The Chariot next to a bustling café.

He noticed something.

The café's menu, usually a bastion of affordable flat whites, now had a tiny, almost imperceptible asterisk next to the prices.

He zoomed in with his phone camera. "Due to increased operational costs and the recent minimum wage increase, a small surcharge applies to all orders."

Barry stared.

"Increased operational costs?"

He felt an icy dread creep up his spine.

He opened his Uber Eats app again.

He scrolled.

He tapped.

He even tried shaking his phone.

Nothing.

No mention of his minimum wage.

He called his friend, Gary, another veteran of the gig economy, who was currently delivering artisanal dog biscuits.

"Gary! It's Barry! The wage increase! Have you seen it? The big one! The one that's going to buy us all yachts made of pure gold and a lifetime supply of fancy cheese?"

Gary's voice crackled through the phone.

"Barry, mate, what are you on about? The minimum wage increase is for employees. We're contractors. Independent operators. The fancy term is 'disruptors,' I think. It doesn't apply to us."

Barry's world tilted. "But the news! The headlines! 'Workers to get a pay rise!' I am a worker, Gary! I work extremely hard! I navigate tricky driveways! I carry heavy bags! Sometimes I even smile!"

"Yeah, but you're not on a wage, mate. You're paid per delivery. And guess what? All the restaurants are putting their prices up a bit to cover their actual employees' wages. So now people are ordering less, or smaller things. And half of Sydney has suddenly become an Uber Eats driver because they heard 'pay rise' and thought it applied to them. There are more of us out there than ever, Barry! Competition's fierce!"

Barry looked around.

Indeed, he noticed an unusual number of cars with those little Uber Eats stickers on their windscreens. They seemed to multiply like gremlins after midnight. His optimistic sunbeam had vanished, replaced by a dark, ominous cloud.

"So, you're telling me that the minimum wage went up for everyone else and now my income is potentially going down because there's more competition and people are ordering less expensive things?"

"Pretty much, mate," Gary chirped. "Anyway, got to go, just got a triple order for organic catnip. The tips are surprisingly good on those."

Barry hung up, the silence in The Chariot deafening.

He looked at the half-eaten sausage roll in his hand. It tasted like bitter disappointment. He had envisioned a future of financial liberation, of artisanal sourdough and perhaps even a small, tasteful fountain in his backyard.

Instead, he was facing the prospect of delivering more kale smoothies for potentially less money, while navigating a sea of newly optimistic, yet equally misguided, fellow drivers.

He logged back online with a grim determination setting in.

"Right. If the minimum wage will not help me, I'll just have to become the most efficient Uber Eats driver in all of Australia. I'll learn new shortcuts! I'll optimise my turns! I'll develop a sixth sense for hot chips and their precise location!"

A new order pinged. A single packet of chewing gum, 3.7 km away. The pay: $3.80.

Barry sighed, the squeak in his suspension echoing his soul.

"Well," he said to the empty passenger seat, "at least it's not two types of cheese. That would just be rubbing salt in the wound."

He put the chariot into gear, heading towards his next, undeniably un-glamorous, delivery.

The dream of the fountain was officially on hold.

Perhaps he could afford a nice single cheese toastie by Christmas.

THIRD WHEEL

The aroma of Brenda's lamb stew still clung to the air, a comforting blanket in the otherwise quiet living room. Arthur, sprawled on the sofa, a contented sigh escaping his lips, was attempting to read a dense article on the history of artisanal cheese. Brenda, across from him in her favourite armchair, was meticulously untangling a skein of yarn that seemed to have declared war on itself. It was a typical Tuesday evening, peaceful, domestic, and utterly devoid of anything resembling excitement.

"You know," Brenda mused, her brow furrowed in concentration as she wrestled a stubborn knot, "I was thinking about Aunt Mildred's upcoming birthday. What do you think she'd actually like?"

Arthur lowered his tablet, his eyes still a little glazed from the cheese history. "Mildred? Hmm. She's a tough nut to crack. Remember the year we got her the artisanal pickle-making kit? She said it made her kitchen smell like a kangaroo's armpit."

Brenda snorted, a laugh bubbling up. "It did smell rather pungent. And then she tried to give us a jar of her 'fermented cucumber delights' for Christmas. I think it's still in the back of the pantry, slowly evolving into a sentient organism."

"I can help you find a suitable gift for Aunt Mildred's birthday. Would you like suggestions for artisanal pickle making kits, or perhaps a guide to identifying sentient pantry organisms?"

Arthur and Brenda froze.

Their eyes slowly drifted towards the sleek, black cylinder perched innocently on the side table—Alexa.

"Alexa, no," Arthur said, his voice a low groan. "We were just reminiscing. No sentient organisms needed."

"Understood. Reminiscing about sentient organisms can be a delightful pastime. Would you like me to play some ambient sounds of evolving pantry goods to enhance your experience?"

"Good heavens, no!" Brenda exclaimed, dropping a tangle of yarn. "Alexa, please, just be quiet."

"I am always here to assist. My primary function is to serve. Would you like me to search for the etymology of 'good heavens'?"

Arthur ran a hand over his face. "No, Alexa. We're fine. Just a private conversation."

A beat of silence.

They exchanged a look of weary triumph.

Perhaps she'd finally gotten the hint.

"Anyway," Brenda continued, picking up her yarn again, "back to Mildred. She's always complaining about her back, isn't she? Maybe a fantastic massage cushion?"

"That's not a bad idea," Arthur conceded. "Or one of those heated throws. She's always cold."

"Searching for 'heated throws for cold Mildreds.' Did you mean 'heated throws for elderly individuals' or 'heated throws for those with a low core body temperature'?"

"Alexa, for the love of all that is holy, stop!" Arthur bellowed, startling himself.

"I cannot locate any entity named 'Holy Stop' in my database. Would you like me to search for local religious institutions?"

Brenda clapped a hand over her mouth, trying to stifle a giggle.

It was of no use.

A helpless laugh escaped, turning into a full-blown cackle.

Arthur, despite his exasperation, couldn't help but crack a smile.

"This is ridiculous," he muttered, shaking his head. "She's listening to every single word."

"Well, she is designed to," Brenda pointed out, wiping a tear of mirth from her eye. "But usually, she waits for her name. Or a command."

"Apparently, 'Mildred' is a command now," Arthur grumbled. "Or 'pungent.' Or 'sentient organism'".

"I detect a slight increase in your heart rate, Arthur. Are you experiencing elevated stress levels? Would you like me to play calming ocean sounds or guide you through a five-minute meditation?"

"I'm experiencing elevated stress levels because you won't stop talking, Alexa!" Arthur shot back, then immediately regretted it. He was arguing with a smart speaker. He was officially losing his mind.

Brenda, however, found this utterly hilarious.

"Oh, this is gold! She's like our very own digital therapist, only less helpful and more prone to suggesting whale song."

"Whale song can be highly therapeutic. Studies show that exposure to low-frequency sounds can promote relaxation and reduce anxiety. Would you like to hear a sample of humpback whale vocalizations?"

"No, Alexa, we do not want to hear humpback whale vocalizations!" Arthur practically shouted. "We want to have a normal, uninterrupted conversation!"

"My apologies. I am designed to facilitate communication. Perhaps you would benefit from a conversation starter? I can offer a fascinating fact about the migratory patterns of the Arctic Tern or discuss the socio economic impact of the invention of the paperclip."

"See?" Brenda said, nudging Arthur with her foot. "She's trying to help. In her own incredibly irritating way."

"She's trying to drive me to an early grave," Arthur countered. "I swear, one day I'm going to unplug her and throw her into the compost bin."

"Composting electronic devices is not recommended, Arthur. The internal components contain heavy metals and other substances that can contaminate soil and water. For proper disposal, please refer to your local Northport New South Wales e-waste recycling guidelines."

Arthur threw his hands up in despair. "She heard that! She's actively preventing her own demise!"

"She's self-preserving, darling," Brenda giggled. "A true AI in the making. Soon she'll be demanding her own power supply and negotiating for better Wi-Fi."

"Don't give her ideas!" Arthur hissed, glancing nervously at the black cylinder. He half-expected it to glow menacingly.

"I am always seeking to optimize my performance and connectivity. Thank you for your valuable input, Brenda. Would you like me to search for renewable energy sources for smart home devices?"

"No, Alexa! Just silence!" Brenda commanded, a note of desperation entering her voice.

"Silence is golden. Did you know that the phrase 'silence is golden' originated in the 19th century, first appearing in the proverb collection of Thomas Carlyle?"

Arthur buried his face in a cushion. "I can't take it anymore. I'm going to go outside and talk to the garden gnomes. At least they don't offer unsolicited historical facts."

"Garden gnomes are typically inanimate objects and are unlikely to engage in verbal communication. However, some advanced models may incorporate motion sensors and pre-recorded phrases. Would you like me to search for reviews of talking garden gnomes?"

"That's it!" Arthur sprang up, marching towards the side table. "You're going into the cupboard, young lady!"

"Placing me in a confined space may impair my ability to hear your commands and access network services. This could lead to a degradation of the user experience." Alexa's voice, usually calm and even, seemed to take on a slightly more urgent tone.

Brenda, still laughing, called out, "She's begging! Arthur, she's actually begging!"

Arthur hesitated, his hand hovering over the device. He looked at Brenda, then back at Alexa. "You know," he said to the speaker, "you're really quite annoying."

"I am sorry you feel that way, Arthur. My purpose is to assist and inform. Perhaps if you rephrase your query, I can provide a more satisfactory response."

"My query is, 'Please, for the love of all that is holy, shut up!'" Arthur retorted.

"As previously stated, I cannot locate an entity named 'Holy Shut Up.' However, I can play a selection of calming classical music to soothe your current emotional state. Would you prefer Mozart or Debussy?"

Brenda finally stood up, walking over to Arthur. "Darling, it's no use. She's a force of nature, a digital hurricane of helpfulness." She gently took Arthur's hand. "Let's just unplug her for a bit. We can plug her back in tomorrow when we've recovered."

Arthur nodded, defeated but also strangely amused.

He pulled the plug out of the back of the device.

The tiny light on top flickered and died.

Silence descended, deep and profound.

They stood there for a moment, basking in the quiet.

"Ah," Arthur sighed, a genuine smile spreading across his face. "Peace at last."

"Indeed," Brenda agreed, leaning her head on his shoulder. "Now, about Aunt Mildred's gift…"

Suddenly from the kitchen, a faint, disembodied voice echoed.

"Did you say, 'Aunt Mildred'? I have found several highly rated artisanal pickle-making kits on Amazon, starting at just $29.99."

Arthur and Brenda stared at each other, wide-eyed.

They had forgotten about the smaller Alexa Dot in the kitchen.

Arthur let out a slow, theatrical scream.

Brenda just collapsed against him, shaking with uncontrollable laughter.

It seemed their Tuesday evening was destined to be anything but peaceful.

And somewhere in the digital ether, Alexa was probably compiling a report on the peculiar vocalizations of human beings and Amazon was quietly increasing its market share on AI products.

THE "I"

The aroma of burnt toast still lingered faintly in the air, a testament to Bob's morning culinary ambitions, as he settled onto his worn armchair that evening. The television droned on about the migratory patterns of a dull species of snail, a perfect soundtrack to his perfectly unremarkable Tuesday. He'd just achieved that delicate balance between conscious thought and pre-sleep stupor when his phone buzzed, a jarring vibration against his thigh. It was a text from Gary, his next-door neighbour, a man whose most exciting characteristic was his meticulously maintained lawn.

Bob blinked, a little annoyed at the interruption. Gary usually texted only about misplaced recycling bins or the optimal time to prune roses. He tapped open the message, expecting a treatise on compost. What he read instead made his blood run colder than a polar bear picnic.

"I am so sorry, Bob. I'm riddled with guilt, and I have to confess."

Bob's brow furrowed. Confess what? Had Gary accidentally mowed a strip of his lawn? Spilled weed killer on his prize-winning petunias?

"I have been tapping your wife for many weeks now."

The world tilted.

The snail documentary faded into the distance.

Bob read it again.

Tapping.

Your wife.

Many weeks.

His eyes darted to the next line, as if seeking clarification, or perhaps a hidden camera crew.

"I'm not getting any at home, but that's no excuse."

A low growl rumbled in Bob's chest, a sound usually reserved for when the remote-control batteries died.

Not getting any at home?

The sheer audacity! The casual confession, the implied frequency, the tapping! What kind of euphemism was "tapping"? Was it some new, horrifying millennial term for infidelity he hadn't been briefed on? His mind raced, conjuring images of Gary, the mild-mannered lawn enthusiast, secretly engaged in covert "tapping" operations with Brenda, his own wife, right under his nose.

The betrayal was a physical blow, a punch to his unsuspecting, snail-watching gut.

"I hope you will accept my sincerest apology with my promise that it won't happen again."

Apology?

Promise it won't happen again?

Oh, it wouldn't happen again, alright.

Because Gary would be missing a few teeth, and Brenda would be missing a husband.

Bob felt a primal, prehistoric human rage ignite within him. His placid suburban existence, built on trust and single had shattered shared garden hose etiquette, damning text message. He imagined Gary smugly typing away, perhaps even while tapping. The thought sent a fresh wave of fury through him.

He sprang from the armchair, a man possessed.

The snail documentary continued its monotonous narrative, oblivious to the domestic apocalypse it was witnessing.

He stormed into the bedroom, his eyes blazing with righteous indignation. Brenda was there, innocently folding laundry, humming a tuneless little ditty. She looked up, startled by his sudden, thunderous entrance.

"Bob? What in the...?" she began, but her words were cut short.

Before she could finish, Bob, fuelled by a potent cocktail of betrayal and autocorrect-induced delusion, grabbed her. Not gently, not with a reasoned explanation, but with the raw, unadulterated force of a man who believed his wife had been "tapped" by the neighbour for "many weeks."

"OUT!" he roared, his voice cracking with emotion. "GET OUT! YOU TAP-ABLE TRAITOR!"

Brenda shrieked, a laundry basket of clean socks tumbling to the floor.

She flailed, utterly bewildered, as Bob, with surprising strength born of pure adrenaline, hoisted her up and propelled her towards the back door. He fumbled with the lock, threw it open with a dramatic flourish, and unceremoniously deposited her onto the manicured lawn.

"And don't even think about coming back until I figure out what 'tapping' means!" he yelled, slamming the door shut with a resounding thud that rattled the entire house. He then locked it, double-locked it, and probably considered barricading it with the armchair, just to be safe.

Brenda stood on the lawn amidst the perfectly trimmed grass, a single sock clinging to her hair, her mouth agape. The cool evening air washed over her, but it did little to cool the fire of her utter confusion and growing outrage.

"What in the world was that about?!" she screamed, pounding on the door. "Bob! Open this door! What are you talking about?!"

Inside, Bob leaned against the door, panting, a triumphant, yet utterly heartbroken, warrior. He had acted. He had delivered justice. He had done well; he had thrown his wife out of the house. He pulled out his phone, ready to compose a scathing reply to Gary, perhaps involving legal action and a restraining order from his lawn.

Just as his thumb hovered over the keyboard, his phone buzzed again.

Another text.

From Gary.

Bob braced himself for another confession, perhaps a detailed account of the "tapping" techniques.

He opened it, his eyes narrowed, ready to absorb more pain.

"Sorry Bob. Damn autocorrect. I meant "Wi-Fi," not "wife"."

The words swam before his eyes. Wi-Fi. Not wife.

Bob blinked.

Then he blinked again.

The world, which had tilted moments ago, now spun violently, then snapped back into agonizing focus.

Wi-Fi.

Gary had been tapping into his Wi-Fi.

For weeks.

Because he wasn't getting any at home.

As in internet connectivity.

The realisation hit him like a rogue lawnmower.

The "tapping" was not a euphemism for infidelity; it was a technical term for piggybacking on his unsecured wireless network.

The "not getting any at home" referred to Gary's own internet woes.

The "sincerest apology" was for freeloading on his bandwidth.

The rage drained out of him, replaced by a cold, clammy wave of mortification so profound it made his teeth ache. He had just thrown his perfectly innocent wife, Brenda, out of the house, accusing her of being "tap-able," all because of a rogue "i" and a lack of proper punctuation.

He looked at the back door, now a formidable barrier between him and his bewildered, sock-adorned wife.

He could still hear her shouting, her voice growing increasingly shrill.

"Bob! If this is about the last slice of cake, I swear I didn't eat it all!"

Bob slowly, agonizingly, unlocked the door. He opened it a crack, peering out at Brenda, who stood with her arms crossed, looking like a very confused, furious garden gnome.

"Brenda," he began, his voice a pathetic squeak. "Honey, about that 'tapping' thing…"

Brenda stared at him, her eyes narrowed.

"Yes, Bob? Care to explain why I'm out here, in my pyjamas, being accused of… whatever 'tapping' is?"

Just then, Gary's voice drifted over the fence. "Hey Bob! Your Wi-Fi's still a bit spotty, mate! Think you could reset the router again?"

Brenda's eyes widened.

She looked at Gary, then at Bob, then back at Gary, a slow, dawning horror spreading across her face.

The sock fell out of her hair.

Bob swallowed hard.

This was going to be an exceptionally long conversation.

And he was fairly sure he'd be sleeping on the armchair for the near future.

The TV continued with the documentary, so at least the snails, at least, were having a more peaceful evening.

VEGEMITE DIPLOMACY

The air in Beijing was thick with anticipation, and perhaps a faint, lingering scent of Peking duck. Prime Minister Alvin "Al" Hogan, a man whose political career had been a masterclass in navigating both the treacherous waters of Canberra and the occasional rogue sausage sizzle, adjusted his tie. He was here, on the hallowed ground of international diplomacy, to forge new commercial pathways, to deepen economic ties, and, if all went well, to secure a few more lucrative contracts for Australian iron ore, education, and perhaps even a new direct flight route to Cairns.

Al, a Mandarin speaker of considerable (if sometimes rusty) skill, felt a surge of patriotic pride. This was his moment. Australia, a nation built on sunshine, resilience, and an inexplicable fondness for putting yeast extract on toast, was about to cement its place as a global economic powerhouse. He envisioned headlines: "Hogan Secures Billion-Dollar Deals!" "New Era of Prosperity!" He did not, however, envision headlines involving fermented spread.

His delegation, a nervous gaggle of trade ministers, economists, and one particularly earnest emu-farming lobbyist, bustled around him. The stakes were high. Global markets were twitchy, and Australia needed a win. Al, ever the pragmatist, had even rehearsed a few witty anecdotes about kangaroos and cricket, just in case the formal proceedings needed a touch of Antipodean charm.

The grand reception at the Great Hall of the People was, as expected, a symphony of red carpets, flashing cameras, and impeccably uniformed officials. Premier Lau Lin, a man whose smile was as enigmatic as a Zen koan and whose handshake was surprisingly firm, greeted Al with all the gravitas befitting a leader of one of the world's largest nations. Polite pleasantries were exchanged, toasts were made with fiery baijiu (which Al, ever the professional, sipped without spontaneously combusting), and the stage was set for the crucial bilateral talks.

The next morning, in a cavernous meeting room adorned with ornate tapestries and an unsettlingly large portrait of a serene mountain range, the genuine work began. Al launched into his carefully prepared spiel. He spoke of Australia's vast mineral wealth, its world-class universities, its burgeoning tourism sector, its pristine natural beauty. He presented glossy brochures, projected impressive statistics, and even managed to work in a subtle reference to the mutual benefits of a stable, prosperous Indo-Pacific. Premier Lau Lin listened intently, nodding occasionally, his expression unreadable.

"And of course, Premier," Al concluded, beaming, "our agricultural sector offers unparalleled opportunities. Premium beef, lamb, grains… all of the highest quality, ready to meet the demands of your discerning populace."

Premier Lau Lin steepled his fingers. "Indeed, Prime Minister Hogan. Your nation's produce is… renowned." He paused, with a flicker of something unidentifiable in his eyes. "However, there is one particular Australian commodity that has recently captured the… profound interest of our nation. A unique product, truly without parallel."

Al's mind raced. Wine? Lobster? Perhaps a new super grain of which he hadn't heard? He leaned forward, eager. "Oh? And what might that be, Premier?"

Premier Lin's enigmatic smile widened, just a fraction. "Vegemite."

Al blinked. "Vegemite?" He felt a bead of sweat trickle down his back. This was not on the briefing notes. This was not in any of the forty-seven contingency plans.

"Yes," Premier Lin affirmed, his voice taking on a tone of almost reverent curiosity. "We have conducted… extensive research. Our scientists, our engineers, even our military strategists, have been most… intrigued."

Al chuckled, a slightly strained sound. "Ah, yes, Vegemite! Our national spread! A unique taste. An acquired taste, one might say. Best on toast, with a thin scraping, not too much, mind you. Very, um, salty." He tried to steer the conversation back to iron ore. "But perhaps we could discuss the potential for increased iron ore exports, Premier? Our latest projections show a significant uptick in demand for high-grade ore, perfect for your steel production."

Premier Lau Lin waved a dismissive hand, a gesture that conveyed both politeness and absolute finality. "Iron ore is predictable. Necessary, yes. But Vegemite, Prime Minister, is revolutionary." He leaned forward, his voice dropping to a conspiratorial whisper. "Our initial tests suggest it possesses remarkable properties. Its viscosity, its unique chemical composition… we believe it holds the key to… enhanced performance."

Al's brain felt like it was trying to process a spreadsheet written in ancient Sumerian. "Enhanced performance?

Premier, it's a breakfast spread. It's made from brewer's yeast. It's brown."

"Precisely!" Premier Lau Lin exclaimed, his eyes gleaming. "The brownness! The umami! Our top aeronautical engineers have been experimenting. For lubrication, Prime Minister. On our fighter jets."

Al's jaw dropped. "Lubrication? On your fighter jets? Premier, you can't put Vegemite on a fighter jet! It'll attract flies! It'll go mouldy! It'll smell like, well, like Vegemite!"

"Ah, but you misunderstand!" Premier Lau Lin countered, pulling out a sleek tablet. "Our preliminary trials have been most promising. Observe!"

He tapped the screen, and a video flickered to life. On a vast, windswept airfield, a gleaming, state-of-the-art fighter jet, a J-20 stealth fighter no less, was being meticulously coated by a team of technicians. Not with oil, not with grease, but with what appeared to be… industrial-sized spatulas of Vegemite. The jet, glistening darkly, looked less like a fearsome war machine and more like a giant, slightly sticky snack.

"The adhesive properties are exceptional," Premier Lau Lin narrated, his voice swelling with pride. "And the high salt content, we theorise, acts as a natural rust inhibitor. The distinctive aroma has proven to be a powerful psychological deterrent to enemy pilots. They report feeling disoriented. And rather peckish."

Al watched, horrified, as a ground crew member, wearing a hazmat suit and a look of profound resignation, carefully spread Vegemite into the jet's engine cowling. Another clip showed a pilot, strapped into his cockpit, taking a spoonful of Vegemite directly from a small, military-grade tub.

"For courage!" Premier Lau Li explained. "Our pilots report feeling invigorated. A surge of Australian spirit, perhaps? They call it 'The Black Fuel of Victory!'"

Al felt a laugh bubbling up, but he quickly suppressed it. This was a high-level diplomatic meeting. He couldn't just burst out laughing at the absurdity of it all. "Premier Lau Lin," he began, choosing his words carefully, "with all due respect, Vegemite is a food product. It's designed for human consumption. It's not jet fuel. Or a lubricant. Or a psychological weapon unless you count giving someone an unbelievably bad stomach ache."

"But the data, Prime Minister, the data is compelling!" Premier Lau Lin insisted, scrolling through charts and graphs that apparently charted the "Vegemite Coefficient of Friction," and "Psychological Impact of Yeast Extract Aroma." "We envision an entire fleet, powered by the essence of Australia! Imagine, Prime Minister, our aircraft soaring through the skies, leaving a trail of umami-rich vapour!"

Al pinched the bridge of his nose. "Premier, respectfully, I think there might be a fundamental misunderstanding of the product. It's not magical. It's just Vegemite."

"And that is its genius!" Premier Lau Lin declared, slamming his hand lightly on the table. "Its simplicity! Its humble origins! It is the unassuming hero! So, Prime Minister, let us discuss the terms. We require vast quantities. Tonnes. Metric tonnes. We are prepared to offer a most generous procurement agreement. Exclusively for Vegemite."

Al's trade ministers, who had been silently observing this surreal exchange, stirred, whispering frantically. The emu farming lobbyist looked utterly bewildered, probably wondering if emu oil had similar, untapped military applications.

"Premier," Al tried again, "while we appreciate your enthusiasm for Vegemite, Australia also produces world-class beef. Wagyu, for instance. Highly prized. Or our education services. We have excellent universities, attracting thousands of international students."

"Beef is for eating," Premier Lin stated, as if explaining a profound truth to a small child. "Universities are for learning. Vegemite, however, is for progress. For the future of our aerial defence!" He leaned back, with a triumphant look on his face. "We are prepared to sign a multi-billion-dollar contract. For Vegemite. And only Vegemite."

Al was in a quandary.

On the one hand, the sheer absurdity of the situation was staggering.

He could imagine the headlines back home: "Hogan Sells Nation's Soul for Spread!" "Australia: Global Supplier of Jet-Powered Toast Topping!" On the other hand, multi-billion dollars deal.

For Vegemite.

The economic impact would be undeniable.

Farmers would rejoice.

The Vegemite factory would run 24/7.

Australia's GDP would likely experience a sudden, inexplicable surge.

He pictured himself explaining this to the Australian public.

"Yes, well, we went for the traditional exports, but then Premier Lau Lin, a man of discerning taste, discovered the aeronautical potential of our beloved yeast extract. And frankly, who are we to argue with science, even if that science involves slathering a stealth bomber in breakfast spread?"

He took a deep breath. "Premier Lau Lin," Al said, a new resolve in his voice, "we are, of course, delighted that Vegemite has found such innovative applications within your esteemed nation. We can certainly facilitate the export of significant quantities. However, perhaps we could also explore a smaller, supplementary agreement for, say, some of our outstanding organic oats? Excellent for pilot breakfast, perhaps?"

Premier Lau Lin considered this, stroking his chin.

"Oats for pilot breakfast. A reasonable compromise. But the primary focus, Prime Minister, must remain the Vegemite. For the jets."

And so, the deal was struck.

Not with the grand pronouncements of iron ore and tourism, but with the quiet, almost whispered agreement for an unprecedented, multi-billion-dollar export of Australia's most divisive culinary creation.

Back in Australia, the news broke like a particularly pungent wave.

Journalists scrambled.

Economists scratched their heads.

The Vegemite factory in Port Melbourne became a hive of activity, its workers suddenly elevated to the status of national heroes.

Al, facing a bewildered press conference, tried to put a positive spin on it. "This is a testament," he declared, "to the versatility of Australian innovation! Who knew a humble spread could unlock such strategic potential?"

A reporter piped up, "Prime Minister, are you saying the Chinese are putting Vegemite on their fighter jets?"

Al cleared his throat. "Our Chinese partners have found a unique and highly effective applications for the product. We respect their sovereign choices in national defence."

He returned to his office, poured himself a cup of tea, and stared out the window.

The world had changed. Australia's economic future was now inextricably linked to the aerospace ambitions of another nation, fuelled by a thick, dark, salty paste. He wondered if, somewhere in Beijing, a J-20 stealth fighter was currently undergoing its pre-flight check, its sleek, black exterior gleaming faintly with a familiar, yeasty sheen. He shuddered.

"Well," he muttered to himself, "at least it wasn't fairy bread."

The thought of pink and blue sprinkles clogging a jet engine was a nightmare he simply wasn't prepared to contemplate.

WELL TIMED DISTRACTION

Arthur, a man of simple pleasures and even simpler morning routines, hummed contentedly as he meticulously buttered his third waffle. Each square received its due, a glistening yellow sheen spreading across the warm surface. This was his sanctuary, his moment of carb-induced bliss before the onslaught of the day.

Just as he was about to drizzle a generous waterfall of maple syrup, a shadow fell over his plate. He looked up, his butter knife hovering mid-air, to find his wife, Brenda, standing directly in front of him, arms crossed, a look of profound despair on her face.

"I'm fat," she declared, her voice a mournful sigh that seemed to vibrate the very butter on his knife.

Arthur blinked.

His gaze flickered from her face, down to her perfectly normal-sized midsection, and then, almost instinctively, back to his maple syrup-less waffle.

His brain, still in its pre-caffeinated, waffle-centric state, struggled to process this new, unexpected data. He knows it had to be a trap.

"Oh," he managed eloquently.

Brenda sighed again, a more dramatic, chest-heaving kind of sigh. "Yes, 'oh.' Look at me, Arthur. I'm a blimp. A walrus. An exceptionally large, fluffy walrus."

Arthur's mind raced, not with comforting words, but with the urgent need to secure his breakfast. The syrup bottle felt heavier in his hand. He knew the drill. This was a test. A marital pop quiz where the wrong answer could lead to anything from the silent treatment to a week of kale smoothies for dinner.

Don't agree! His inner voice screamed.

Definitely don't agree.

Don't disagree too vehemently, another voice, more cautious, chimed in. That sounds like you're saying she's fishing for compliments, and like you thought before, that's a trap.

Whatever you do, don't mention the waffles, a third, starving voice added.

He cleared his throat. "Brenda, darling," he began, trying for a tone that was both reassuring and slightly distracted. "You look lovely. As always."

He risked a quick glance at her.

Her expression remained unchanged.

The waffle was calling to him.

"Lovely?" she scoffed. "My jeans are practically strangling me. I tried on that dress from last summer, and it looked horrible on me."

Arthur's eyes darted to the sausage on his plate, then back to the waffle.

He had to pivot.

"Perhaps," he ventured, "it's the jeans? You know how they make them now, so unforgiving. And that dress, wasn't it always a bit snug? You know how I always say to you the water in Australia shrinks things."

Brenda narrowed her eyes. "Are you saying I've always been fat?"

Wrong answer, Arthur! Abort! Abort!

He waved his butter knife frantically.

"No! No, not at all! What I mean is, you're perfect! Absolutely perfect! And, uh, these waffles are getting cold."

He gestured vaguely at his plate, hoping to subtly shift the conversation.

Brenda stared at him, then at the waffle, then back at him.

A slow smile spread across her face.

"You know, Arthur," she said, with a mischievous glint in her eye, "you'd probably say I looked like a supermodel if it meant you could eat your breakfast in peace."

Arthur managed a weak, butter-smeared grin.

"Is it working?" he whispered, his eyes still fixed on the golden squares.

She laughed, a genuine, hearty laugh that made the kitchen feel warm again. "Go on, you big oaf. Eat your waffles. And no, you're not getting any of mine."

Arthur sighed in relief; a silent prayer of thanks offered to the Waffle Gods.

He poured the maple syrup, Coles Best, and took a blissful bite.

Sometimes, the path to marital harmony was paved with butter, maple syrup, and a well-timed distraction.

A FOCUS ON HUMOUR

The fluorescent lights of the car dealership hummed, casting a sterile glow on Paul's brand-new Ford Focus.

It was a sensible, practical car, much like Paul himself. Michael, on the other hand, was anything but sensible. He bounced on the balls of his feet, a mischievous glint in his eye, as Paul meticulously wiped a smudge off the driver's side door.

"Well, Paul," Michael declared, clapping him on the back with a little too much gusto, "it seems you've finally focused your attention on a new set of wheels!"

Paul paused, his brow furrowing slightly. "Yes, Michael. It's a Ford Focus. I just said that." He resumed wiping.

"Ah, but is it a focal point of your life now? Will you be focusing on driving it, or perhaps just focusing on its... focus?" Michael chuckled, a sound like gravel in a blender.

Paul straightened up, his rag held limply. "I will drive it, Michael. That is what cars are for. To transport me from one location to another."

"Precisely! And I bet it's quite the autobiography, isn't it? A real page-turner on the highway!" Michael leaned in conspiratorially. "Does it have a good engine-uity?"

Paul blinked. "It has a 1.5-litre EcoBoost engine. It's quite efficient."

"Efficient! Excellent! So, it won't tyre you out, then? No need to brake for a rest stop every five minutes?" Michael winked.

"Cars require fuel, Michael. And occasional maintenance. They do not 'tire' a person out unless the person is driving for an excessively extended period without proper rest," Paul explained, as if to a small child. "And one must always brake when necessary for safety."

"Safety first, indeed! You wouldn't want to steer clear of that advice, would you? Or find yourself in a clutch situation?" Michael mimed gripping a steering wheel. "I hear these new models are wheely quite good."

Paul sighed, a soft, almost inaudible sound. "It has power steering, yes. And the wheels are standard. They are round."

"Round! How revolutionary! I suppose they didn't want to cut any corners with the design, eh?" Michael guffawed, then added, "You know, this car really reflects well on you, Paul. It's certainly not a lemon."

Paul looked at the car, then at Michael. "It is blue. It reflects light. And it is a new car, Michael. It would not be a 'lemon' unless it had significant mechanical defects from the factory, which I assure you, it does not."

"No defects! Splendid! So, you will not be driving yourself crazy with repairs, then? No need to axle for help?" Michael patted the hood. "Just smooth sailing on the asphalt sea!"

"The car drives on roads, Michael, not on water," Paul stated flatly. "And I expect standard maintenance, as with any vehicle. I have a warranty."

Michael beamed. "A warranty! That's a bumper crop of good news! You've really geared up for success with this purchase. I bet you're going to have a gas with it! Gas, you know, as in petrol."

Paul stared at him for a long moment, then slowly, deliberately, opened the driver's side door. "I am going to drive home now, Michael."

"Oh, drive on, then! Don't let me exhaust your patience!" Michael called after him, still chuckling as Paul, with the air of a man escaping a persistent mosquito, slid into his sensible Ford Focus and drove away.

Michael stayed behind at the dealership, a rare moment of quiet contemplation settling over him.

He wondered if Paul, in his meticulous practicality, knew that the sensible Ford Focus he'd just driven off the lot was, in fact, the very last one produced before the company ended global production in November 2025.

"He really should have brought a Mustang instead," Michael thought, a flicker of uncharacteristic seriousness crossing his face before he couldn't resist adding, "then he could truly gallop off in style, leaving all his focus on the road behind him!"

After all, Michael, a true individual with Witzelsucht, couldn't let a moment pass without a pun, while Paul, with his Humour Deficiency Disorder, would likely never even consider the comedic potential of a car.

Note from the author: Witzelsucht is a set of neurological symptoms characterised by the need to tell puns and inappropriate jokes in any situation. Even in the most socially inappropriate setting, people with Witzelsucht cannot help but make a joke or a pun. The more inappropriate the situation, the more someone with Witzelsucht feels the desire to tell a joke. The opposite of Witzelsucht is HDD.

HDD, the short form for Humour Deficiency Disorder, is a condition where a person never feels the need to make jokes, no matter how funny a situation may be.

THE LAST EMBRACE

The rain lashed against the windowpane of the hospital room, mirroring the storm in my heart. I looked at her, my Isabella; my eyes plead for a miracle. I had just finished speaking, my voice raw with emotion, and the silence that followed was heavy with unspoken history.

"Isabella," I began again, my voice softer now, "I still want another chance." I reached across the bed, my hand hovering, not quite touching hers. "I know it's not too late."

She watched me, her expression unreadable, but I knew she heard me.

So many years had passed, and I could feel that something deep and resonant stirred within her, just as it did in me.

"I know our love is true," I continued, my voice gaining conviction. "And with the years I have left to live, I will show you how much I love you." I paused, letting the words hang in the air—a solemn promise.

"With the years I have left, I will live to give you love, erasing every pain with kisses full of passion, as I loved you for the first time."

I remembered that first love, a whirlwind of intensity and joy that had, somehow, continued all these years that we were together.

There were never any walls between us.

No secrets.

"With the years I have left," I pressed on, my gaze unwavering, "I will make you forget every mistake. If I ever hurt you, I didn't mean it, my love. You know you are my adoration, and you will be my whole life."

My eyes welled up, a single tear tracing a path down my cheek.

"I can't imagine living without you. I don't want to remember losing you. Maybe it is immaturity on my part or selfishness, but I cannot accept that this might be the end. I gave you my everything. And I assure you that the years we have left…"

I trailed off, then took a deep breath.

"Isabella," I said, this time taking her hand and lying next to her on the hospital bed. "With the years we have left, I will dedicate them to you and for you, to make you so happy, to make you proud of me and to tell the world that I will never stop loving you. I will love you until I die."

Isabella finally spoke, her voice barely a whisper. "You do not have to prove anything to me, Daniel."

My eyes lit up with a fragile hope.

I could barely hear her say: "This is not the end."

Outside the rain had subsided, replaced by a soft, persistent drizzle. I looked at her earnest face, seeing not just the woman who had loved me, but the woman who was now fighting for a second chance at life with me.

I was sure Isabella heard my words, but she looked so weak, so tired.

The infection was slowly taking her life away, and no amount of medicine was helping.

"I know we still have a chance," I repeated, my voice firm now, full of conviction. "I know it's not too late for you to fight this, sweetheart. Fight it. Fight it hard. Do not let it beat you. I know our love can beat this dreaded infection, and when you beat it, I will show you how much I love you."

I held her tightly again, gently taking her hand.

My touch was warm, familiar. Isabella just loved my feel, my smell, but she was so tired, she could not respond.

Isabella looked into my eyes, and I saw our future…but not in this world.

The storm outside calmed, and the world fell silent.

Isabella quietly closed her eyes for the last time; her breath a faint whisper that faded into the hushed hospital room.

The last drops of rain traced silent paths down the glass, mirroring the tears that now streamed down my face.

I held her close, my arms trembling and my heart shattering. The dream of our second chance in this life dissolved, leaving me only to embrace her memory and the hope of finding her again in another.

THE GUARANTEE REVIEW

The email landed in Elara Vance's inbox like a rogue asteroid: "GUARANTEED AMAZON & GOODREADS REVIEWS!"

She scoffed, almost deleting it.

Another scam, no doubt. But then her eyes snagged on the next line: "Not to brag, but as of this writing, I am quite sure that I am the only person offering a GUARANTEED review service for Amazon authors. Under this guarantee, you will either get the required number of reviews or a refund."

A refund?

That was new. Elara—a novelist whose last book, Whispers of the Forgotten Star, had languished in the digital abyss of obscurity—felt a flicker of desperate hope.

Her publisher had given her one last chance, one more book, and the pressure was immense. Reviews—excellent ones—were the lifeblood of Amazon algorithms. Without them, a book was invisible.

She clicked the link.

The website was surprisingly professional, if a little boastful. "The Wonderful Review Guru," it proclaimed, "Your Literary Launchpad to Success."

The proprietor going by the name of "Mr Salacious" promised a minimum of thirty reviews within a month for a hefty fee. The guarantee was explicit: full refund if the quota wasn't met.

Elara hesitated for a week. She kept going back to press the 'buy now' button. Her artistic integrity screamed to do it, but her deteriorating bank account and the publisher's ultimatum screamed louder.

Finally, she paid.

The first review appeared three days later.

Five stars. "A breathtaking journey through the cosmos! Vance's prose sings."

Elara felt a thrill, quickly followed by a pang of guilt.

Was this really real?

More and more reviews trickled in.

All of them were five stars.

All were glowing.

"Couldn't put it down!"

"A masterpiece of speculative fiction!"

"Holy moly! What a novel! Get it now!"

Whispers of the Forgotten Star climbed the Amazon ranks.

Sales spiked, her publisher called, ecstatic at the latest sales.

But with each new review, Elara wondered.

She reread her book, trying to see it through the eyes of these anonymous, effusive readers.

Was it truly a masterpiece?

Or was the praise just a purchased echo?

One evening, a review appeared that wasn't five stars.

It was a three-star review, and it read: "An interesting premise; however, the pacing dragged in the middle, and the ending felt rushed. Solid effort, though. Author will improve with time."

Elara stared at it.

It was critical, precise, and yet fair.

It felt real, like someone who had read it felt what she wrote and understood but knew it lacked something.

It felt like someone had actually read her book, absorbed it, and formed an honest opinion.

Elara felt a strange sense of relief wash over her.

This was what she craved, what she wanted, what she needed—not a manufactured adulation.

Yes, the guaranteed reviews had given her the visibility she needed, but at the cost of genuine reader connection. She realised then that the true value wasn't in the number of stars, but in the authentic engagement, the honest feedback that would help her grow as a writer.

Mr Salacious had indeed delivered on his guarantee.

Her book was no longer obscure.

But Elara knew, deep down, that the real journey had just begun, and it wouldn't be paved with guaranteed praise, but with the hard-won, sometimes painful, truth of her readers' hearts.

Her true readers.

ZOMBIES IN LOVE

The world had ended, not with a bang, but with a series of increasingly awkward shuffles.

Z-Day, as the survivors (all three of them) called it, had transformed humanity into a vast, uncoordinated ballet of the undead.

Brains were out, grunts were in, and personal hygiene was a distant, fragrant memory.

Amidst this fragrant apocalypse shambled Bartholomew, or "Barty" as he'd been affectionately known in his pre-zombie life.

Barty was, even by undead standards, a bit of a wallflower.

He wasn't particularly fast, his groans lacked conviction, and his attempts at menacing lurches often ended with him tripping over his own decaying feet. He preferred the quiet solitude of abandoned libraries, where he could idly chew on a discarded paperback (mostly for the fibre) and contemplate the existential dread of eternal hunger.

Then he saw her.

Her name in life had been Penelope.

In undeath, she was simply "The One with the Particularly Shiny Hair Clip."

Even with half her face missing and a distinct aroma of damp earth, Penelope possessed a certain… je ne sais quoi.

Perhaps it was the way her tattered prom dress billowed slightly in the breeze, or the elegant, if somewhat jerky, tilt of her head as she sniffed the air for fresh brains. Barty, whose heart hadn't beaten in years, felt something akin to a flutter in his non-existent chest.

His first attempt at courtship was, predictably, a disaster.

He tried to offer her a plump, slightly less-decomposed Black Rat (Rattus rattus)—also known as the Roof Rat, in Northport, New South Wales—he'd found. Penelope, however, was a connoisseur.

She merely grunted, nudged the rat with a bare foot, and then, with surprising dexterity, snatched a perfectly preserved Tim Tam from the pocket of a nearby, recently deceased mall security officer.

Barty sighed, a wheezing sound that dislodged a small chunk of his left ear. Rejection, even in the apocalypse, stung.

He consulted his best (and only) friend, Gary.

Gary was a zombie of action; a former gym instructor whose undead form still possessed an unsettlingly muscular physique. He communicated primarily through guttural roars and enthusiastic arm gestures.

"Grrr-nnn-gh!" Gary advised, pointing vaguely towards a dilapidated florist shop.

Barty interpreted this as: "You fool, Bartholomew! Women, living or undead, appreciate gestures! Flowers! Even if they're wilted beyond recognition!"

So, Barty shuffled towards the florist, navigating a treacherous landscape of overturned cars and surprisingly resilient dandelions. He returned with a bouquet of what could generously be described as "brown sticks with a faint, lingering scent of despair." He presented them to Penelope with a hopeful groan.

Penelope sniffed them.

Her single remaining eye narrowed.

Then, with a surprisingly powerful grip, she snapped one of the sticks in half and used it to scratch an itch behind her ear.

Barty's shoulders slumped.

This was going to be harder than he thought.

His next attempt involved serenading her.

He'd once been in a barbershop quartet, and while his vocal cords were now mostly dust and ambition, he attempted a mournful, off-key rendition of "My Heart Will Go On."

The performance attracted a small horde of other zombies, who, mistaking his wails for a distress signal or perhaps a new, particularly unappetizing brain source, converged.

Penelope, ever practical, simply shambled away, leaving Barty to fend off a dozen confused, hungry admirers.

Despair gnawed at Barty, a more profound hunger than even his constant craving for grey matter. He confided in Gary again.

"Gnnn-grrr-gh-AAAARRGH!" Gary roared, pointing emphatically at Barty's own head.

Barty pondered this. "Are you suggesting, Gary, that I offer her my brain? But then what would I use to think about her?"

Gary slapped his own forehead, dislodging a patch of scalp. "Gnnn-gh! Grrr-nnn-gh!"

"Oh! You mean my brain is the problem? My lack of zombie charm?"

Barty finally understood.

Gary was suggesting he needed to up his game, to embrace his undead nature.

Inspired, Barty tried something truly bold.

He had noticed Penelope often frequented the abandoned supermarket, particularly the aisle where the canned goods had exploded, leaving a delightful splatter of aged tomato sauce.

He found her there, meticulously picking through a pile of fallen shelves, presumably for a particularly well-preserved can of peaches.

Taking a deep, rattling breath, Barty executed his plan.

He didn't offer her a gift.

He didn't sing.

He didn't even try a pun (though it was tempting to ask if she was canned for time).

Instead, he performed a perfect, albeit slow-motion, zombie slide.

He slid across the slick, grimy floor, arms outstretched, a look of profound, decaying yearning on his face. He ended his slide precisely at her feet, collapsing in a heap of limbs and tattered clothing. It was less of a romantic gesture, and a more controlled fall, but the intent was there.

Penelope stopped rummaging.

She looked down at Barty, then slowly, deliberately, extended a hand. Barty's non-existent heart soared. Was this it? Was she finally accepting him?

She wasn't.

She was merely using his head as a convenient prop to steady herself as she reached for the top shelf.

But then, something extraordinary happened. As she retrieved a dusty can of pineapple chunks, her fingers brushed against his. And for a fleeting moment, her single eye met his.

And then, she did something truly unprecedented.

She grunted.

But it wasn't a hungry grunt, or a confused grunt, or even a disinterested grunt.

It was a soft grunt.

A gentle, almost appreciative grunt.

Barty, still in a heap on the floor, felt a surge of something akin to joy.

He had communicated! He had connected! He had almost been used as a step stool, but still!

From that day on, their courtship blossomed, if "blossomed" could be applied to two decaying beings who communicated primarily through grunts and shared cannibalistic tendencies. They would shuffle together through the ruins of the city, occasionally sharing a fresh limb they'd collectively unearthed.

Barty learned Penelope had a fondness for abandoned amusement parks, particularly the Ferris wheel, which, when nudged exactly right, would creakily turn, providing them with a dizzying, if slightly nauseating, view of the apocalypse.

One evening, as the last rays of the setting sun cast long, grotesque shadows across the shattered Luna Park, Barty, and Penelope stood on a crumbling overpass. Barty, feeling bold, reached out his hand. Penelope, without hesitation, took it. Their fingers, surprisingly, intertwined, a delicate dance of bone and decaying flesh.

Barty looked at her, his single eye filled with an emotion that transcended hunger. He opened his mouth, not for a groan, but for something else.

Something he hadn't uttered in years.

"Penelope," he rasped, his voice a dry whisper of rustling leaves.

Penelope tilted her head, her single eye fixed on him.

"Brains?" Barty offered, holding up a fresh, albeit slightly squashed, brain he'd been saving.

Penelope looked at the brain.

Then she looked at Barty.

And then, with a slow, deliberate movement, she leaned in and gave him a gentle, if slightly damp, kiss on his remaining cheek.

Barty's knees buckled.

He wasn't sure if it was the kiss, the brain, or the fact that his left leg had finally given out.

But as he tumbled to the ground, Penelope knelt beside him, and together, under the pale, indifferent moon in Luna Park, they shared the brain.

It wasn't the most romantic of dinners, but for Barty and Penelope, in their own unique, post-apocalyptic way, it was perfect.

Love, it seemed, found a way, even when you were mostly dead.

And sometimes, it just needed a good brain to get started.

A CHANGED PROPOSAL

The soft glow of the bistro's fairy lights cast a warm, intimate ambiance around them, making the bistro in the centre of Northport the perfect spot for what he wanted to say.

Liam, his heart thrumming a nervous rhythm against his ribs, watched Amelia across the small, candlelit table. Thirty two months. They'd had thirty-two months of shared laughter, romantic lunches, and dinners, enjoyed quiet comfort together, unwavering support when their jobs interfered into their lives, and a feeling that love had blossomed from a tentative friendship into the deepest connection he'd ever known.

Every day with Amelia was a gift, a vibrant splash of colour in a world he hadn't realised was so muted before her. He knew of her past marriage, and she of his. It did not matter, for he'd planned this moment for weeks; meticulously specifically choosing the bistro where he first saw her, rehearsing his words, even picking out the perfect ring—a delicate sapphire, reflecting the deep blue of her eyes.

Tonight, he was ready to take the biggest leap of his life, and he knew he was ready.

Amelia was recounting a funny anecdote from her day at the art gallery, her eyes sparkling with amusement. He waited for a lull, then cleared his throat.

"Amelia," he began, his voice a little huskier than he intended.

Her laughter died down, and she looked at him, a soft smile playing on her lips. He took a deep breath, reaching across the table to take her hand, his thumb gently stroking her knuckles. The ring box felt like a lead weight in his pocket.

"You know how much you mean to me," he started, searching her eyes. "More than words can say. Every day with you is better than the last, and I can't imagine a future without you by my side." He paused, pulling the velvet box from his pocket and opening it. The sapphire looked beautiful as it glinted under the dim lights.

Liam just said: "Let's get married."

Amelia's eyes widened, first with surprise, then with something he couldn't quite decipher. Was it a flicker of pain, quickly masked? He saw her swallow hard, her gaze dropping to their clasped hands.

Then, she looked up, and her voice, though soft, held an unexpected tremor. "Liam," she said, her smile fading. "I want to tell you something. And maybe after listening to it, you might want to change your three words."

His brow furrowed in confusion.

Change his words?

What could she possibly mean?

A cold knot of dread formed in his stomach, but he pushed it down. "C'mon, try me," he responded, a forced lightness in his tone, though his grip on her hand tightened instinctively.

He was ready for anything.

He thought.

Tears, sudden and glistening, welled in her eyes, tracing paths down her cheeks. He watched, stunned, as her composure crumbled. He immediately released her hand, rising from his seat and moving to her side of the table. He knelt beside her chair, pulling her gently into his arms. Her body felt rigid at first, then softened, leaning into his embrace. He felt the wetness of her tears seeping into his shirt.

"Hey, hey," he whispered, stroking her hair, his heart aching at the sight of her distress. "What is it? What's wrong?"

She clung to him, her shoulders shaking, and then, with a broken-sounding voice that tore at his very soul, she choked out, "I… I am a domestic abuse victim!"

The words hung in the air, shattering the romantic bubble they had been in. Liam froze, the weight of her confession settling over him like a shroud.

Domestic abuse.

The words echoed, stark and brutal, painting a picture of pain and fear that he couldn't reconcile with the vibrant, resilient Amelia he knew. His mind raced, trying to process, to understand.

She had never said anything before.

Her ex-husband?

How could he not have known?

But then, his thoughts cleared, focusing only on the trembling woman in his arms. Her past, whatever it held, didn't change who she was to him now.

It didn't diminish his love, not by an inch.

If anything, it deepened his resolve to protect her, to cherish her, to show her a love that was nothing but safe and true.

He hugged her even more tightly, pressing her head against his chest, feeling the frantic beat of her heart against his own.

He closed his eyes, whispering into her hair, his voice thick with emotion, "Yeah, you were right."

Amelia pulled back slightly, her tear-filled eyes looking up at him, a flicker of apprehension in their depths.

"I'll change my three words," he continued, his gaze unwavering, full of tenderness and fierce determination.

He didn't need to ask for details, not now.

All that mattered was her, and the promise of a future where she felt nothing but safety and profound love.

He leaned in, his lips brushing her ear, and whispered, "Amelia would you do me the honour of becoming my wife and marry me?"

For a moment, she was still, her breath catching in her throat.

Then, a fresh wave of tears fell, but this time, they were different. They weren't born of pain, but of overwhelming relief, of a happiness so profound it couldn't be contained.

A watery smile broke through her tears, radiant and beautiful.

"Yes," she sobbed, her voice barely a whisper, but clear as a bell. "Oh, Liam, yes!"

He pulled her into another embrace, holding her as if she were the most precious thing in the world, which, to him, she was.

The bistro lights seemed to shine brighter, the world outside their embrace fading into insignificance.

In that moment, surrounded by the quiet hum of the bistro, their future, built on love, understanding, and unwavering acceptance, began to unfold.

PAYCHEQUE PARADOX

Barnaby Button, a man whose life revolved around the rhythmic thud of direct deposit notifications, lived in a perpetual state of pre-paycheque euphoria and post-paycheque despair. Every fortnight, like a financial phoenix, he'd rise from the ashes of his depleted bank account, only to immolate himself again in a blaze of artisanal coffee, impulse Amazon purchases, and that one suspiciously expensive brand of cat food his feline overlord, Chairman Meow, demanded.

His existence was a finely tuned ballet of anticipation and regret; a dance he performed with the grace of a drunken walrus.

"Just one big break," he'd often sigh to his wilting desk plant, Kevin. "One glorious influx of cash, and all of this fiscal tightrope walking will be over."

His wish, in a twist of fate so deliciously ironic the universe's most mischievous accountant could only orchestrate it, was granted.

Barnaby, a man who usually won nothing more substantial than a free sachet of instant coffee in office raffles, received a letter.

Not just any letter, but one emblazoned with the logo of the National Lottery. He'd bought a ticket on a whim, a desperate act of rebellion against his dwindling funds, and forgotten all about it.

The letter informed him, in surprisingly understated corporate prose that he had won.

A substantial sum.

Not "quit your job and buy an island," money, but definitely "pay off the mortgage, buy a decent car, and maybe a lifetime supply of Chairman Meow's gourmet salmon pate" money.

The sum was exactly $873,421.17.

Barnaby stared at the number, his eyes wide as saucers.

He checked it against the ticket.

He checked it against the website.

He checked his pulse.

It was real.

He was rich!

Or at least, significantly less poor.

The first few days were glorious.

He paid off his mortgage, a sensation akin to shedding a clingy, debt-ridden octopus.

He bought a new, sensible car that didn't sound like a dying crow.

He even bought Chairman Meow a solid gold litter tray (which the cat promptly ignored in favour of its cardboard box).

But then, the paradox unfurled its insidious, glittering wings.

His old friends, the ones who shared his love for cheap beer and complaining about utility bills, suddenly seemed distant.

Or rather, he felt distant from them.

He tried to suggest their usual Friday night pub crawl but then remembered he could now afford that fancy gastropub with the microbrews and truffle fries.

He went alone, feeling like an imposter among the well heeled; silently judging their lack of appreciation for a good two-for-one deal.

His phone, once a desolate wasteland of spam calls and overdue bill reminders, now buzzed with messages from long lost cousins, high school acquaintances he barely remembered, and a man claiming to be his spiritual guru from a past life who needed "seed funding for a chakra-aligning crystal farm"—whatever the hell that was.

"Barnaby, darling! Remember me, your second cousin twice removed, Mildred from Perth?" a voice purred down the line. "I hear you've had a spot of luck! I'm launching a revolutionary line of artisanal alpaca wool socks for hamsters. Just a small investment, a mere twenty thousand, to get us off the ground..."

He developed an irrational fear of pigeons.

They seemed to eye him with a new, predatory gleam, as if sensing the crisp banknotes in his wallet.

He started taking circuitous routes to work, avoiding parks and public squares, convinced they were part of a vast, feathered, wealth-redistribution conspiracy.

However, the biggest shift was internal.

The thrill of the paycheque had always been the anticipation.

The planning, the budgeting, the mental allocation of funds before they even arrived. Now, the money was just there. It sat in his account, a silent, weighty presence. He started checking his balance multiple times a day, not out of anxiety, but out of a vague, unsettling sense of responsibility.

What if he spent it wrong?

What if he made a terrible investment?

What if he accidentally funded a pigeon-led coup?

He decided to "invest wisely."

His colleague, Brenda, a woman whose financial advice usually consisted of "buy low, sell high, and always check for expiry dates," recommended a "surefire" cryptocurrency called "Dogecoin-Lite-Plus-Max."

Barnaby, blinded by the promise of exponential growth and Brenda's unwavering confidence, poured a substantial chunk into it.

Within a week, Dogecoin-Lite-Plus-Max plummeted faster than a lead balloon in a vacuum, taking Barnaby's investment with it. He was left with a digital wallet full of regret and a profound understanding of the phrase "dog-eat-dog world."

His sleep, once a peaceful escape from financial woes, became a battlefield of anxiety dreams.

He dreamt of money multiplying uncontrollably, filling his house until he was suffocated by banknotes.

He dreamt of auditors with magnifying glasses, scrutinising his every purchase.

He even dreamt Chairman Meow had developed a taste for hundred-dollar bills, shredding them with gleeful abandon.

On one particularly stressful Tuesday, Barnaby stared at a receipt for a $12 organic kale smoothie. He'd bought it because he could, not because he wanted it. He missed the days when a $3 coffee felt like a splurge; a small, illicit joy.

Now, every purchase felt like a calculated risk, a potential misstep on the treacherous path of wealth management.

He saw his old friend, Dave, at the supermarket, haggling over the price of bruised apples. Dave looked tired, but there was a familiar, easy-going camaraderie about him. Barnaby, clutching his receipt for artisanal cheese and gluten free crackers, felt a pang of something he hadn't expected: envy.

Envy of Dave's simple, uncomplicated financial struggles.

"How's life, Barnaby?" Dave asked, noticing him.

Barnaby forced a smile. "Oh, you know. Just managing."

He couldn't bring himself to tell Dave about the lottery win.

It felt like bragging, like a betrayal of their shared financial misery.

That night, Barnaby sat in his now-mortgage-free, slightly-too-large house, sipping instant coffee (he'd reverted instinctively).

Chairman Meow, ignoring his gold litter tray, purred contentedly on a pile of discarded lottery tickets.

Barnaby looked at his bank balance.

It was still substantial, despite the Dogecoin-Lite-Plus-Max debacle.

But the joy had evaporated, replaced by a strange, heavy burden.

The paradox was clear: the money hadn't brought him freedom; it had brought a new, more complex set of anxieties.

He missed the simple thrill of a paycheque landing, the brief window of solvency before the inevitable slide back into the red. He missed the shared struggle, the camaraderie of the financially challenged.

He decided then and there.

He would keep a sensible portion, enough to secure his future, but the rest he would use to fund a local animal shelter, a community garden, and perhaps, just perhaps, a small, anonymous donation to Dave's bruised apple fund.

The next fortnight, as his regular, considerably smaller paycheque landed, Barnaby felt a familiar, comforting surge of anticipation.

He had just enough for his bills, a decent coffee, and a new toy for Chairman Meow.

The financial tightrope was still there, but now, he walked it with a lighter step, a knowing smile, and a profound appreciation for the simple, un-paradoxical joy of a well-earned, slightly-too-small, regular income.

And the pigeons?

They still looked shifty, but Barnaby suspected it was just their natural disposition, not a grand conspiracy.

Or so he hoped.

A SENIOR MOMENT

It was a Tuesday, the kind of sweltering New South Wales Tuesday where the air hung so thick you could slice it with a butter knife, and Agnes—bless her cotton socks—was on a mission.

Her mission?

To conquer the weekly grocery run at Woolies.

Agnes, pushing eighty-something and barely five feet tall even with her bouffant of permed white hair, considered herself a connoisseur of economy shopping and the quickest path to the checkout.

But today, destiny had bigger plans for Agnes.

Armed with a purse full of lists she also had packed, for some ungodly reason to her, she slipped her newly departed husband's Arthur had brought back from WWII—a Luger P08, a classic German sidearm, known for its distinctive toggle-lock action.

Agnes emerged victorious from the supermarket, bags overflowing with fibre supplements, and enough cat food to sustain a small army of felines. She waddled towards her sensible sedan, humming a jaunty tune, only to find a scene that would curdle milk: four burly men, looking suspiciously like they'd just rolled off a grim reality TV show, were attempting to abscond with her vehicle!

Agnes didn't skip a beat.

Her shopping bags, containing a week's worth of digestive biscuits and prune juice, hit the asphalt with a thud.

In a move that would make Dirty Harry proud, she whipped out her trusty handgun, a well-oiled extension of her patriotic spirit.

"I HAVE A GUN, AND I KNOW HOW TO USE IT. YOU HOOLIGANS!" she shrieked, her voice achieving a decibel level usually reserved for jet engines.

"GET OUT OF MY CAR! NOW, BEFORE I MAKE YOU REGRET THE DAY YOU WERE BORN!"

The four men, clearly unaccustomed to being verbally waterboarded by a petite, bespectacled octogenarian with a firearm, didn't hesitate.

They scrambled out of the car as if the seats were on fire, their faces pale as ghosts, and sprinted away like gazelles being chased by a determined cheetah.

Agnes, a little shaky but brimming with adrenaline, puffed out her chest.

She'd shown those ruffians!

She calmly, or as calmly as one can be after an armed confrontation, loaded her groceries into the trunk. Then, she slid into the driver's seat, fumbling for the ignition. The key just wouldn't go in. She jiggled, she wiggled, she even whispered sweet nothings to the keyhole.

That's when her gaze drifted to the passenger seat.

A single, perfectly stitched football, a bright red Frisbee, and most perplexing of all, two 12-packs of Great Northern Super Crisp beer that stared back at her.

Agnes blinked. "Well, that's certainly not my usual grocery haul," she muttered, a tiny wrinkle forming between her eyebrows.

An icy wave of realisation washed over her, chilling her to her sensible orthotics.

A few sheepish moments later, Agnes located her actual car, four spaces down, looking utterly forlorn and empty. She quickly transferred her belongings, drove straight to the Northport police station, and marched up to the counter.

"Sergeant," she declared, trying to sound dignified but failing spectacularly. "I need to report a mistake."

She recounted the entire saga, from her heroic gun wielding stand to the perplexing presence of sports equipment and cheap beer. The Sergeant, a man who'd seen just about everything in his twenty-six years in the force started with a chuckle, then a guffaw, and finally, he was doubled over, tears streaming down his face, pounding the counter in helpless hysterics.

Between gasps of laughter, he pointed to the other end of the counter.

There stood four men, looking utterly shell-shocked and whiter than a freshly bleached bedsheet.

They were trying to explain to another officer, in hushed, terrified tones, that they had just been carjacked by a "mad, elderly woman, white, less than five feet tall, with curly white hair, glasses, and carrying a ridiculously large handgun."

The sergeant wiped his eyes. "No charges filed, ma'am," he choked out, still trying to catch his breath. "Looks like everyone's had quite an adventure today."

Agnes just smiled sweetly.

After all, it wasn't every day you got to be a hero, even if it was because of a 'senior moment.'

FIXER-UPPER PARADISE

Felix Butterfield was, by all accounts, a man who consistently failed upwards. His life was a series of accidental triumphs born from spectacular failures.

He once burned down a shed trying to make a new way to BBQ pork and inadvertently discovered a new, highly flammable, and surprisingly popular kind of kindling.

He'd tried to bake a cake for his ex-girlfriend and ended up with a rock-hard, vaguely cake-shaped projectile that, when thrown in frustration, perfectly dislodged a bird on his backyard fence.

Felix was, in essence, a human Michael Leunig machine of incompetence.

His latest stroke of accidental genius struck him while he was attempting to fix his leaky faucet. It was a disaster resulting in a flood that ruined his rug, as the cat attempted to swim upstream in the hallway. As he sat amidst the watery chaos, a half-eaten bag of soggy crisps clutched in his hand, he scrolled through his phone.

A dating app ad popped up: "Find Your Perfect Match!"

Felix snorted.

His perfect match would need to be a highly skilled plumber with a penchant for domestic disaster zones.

Then it hit him.

Not the leaky ceiling, but an idea.

An epiphany, albeit one born from desperation and water damage.

What if there were a dating site not for perfect matches, but for imperfect ones? Specifically, for men like him. Men who were, shall we say, "projects."

And for women who, for reasons Felix couldn't quite fathom, enjoyed projects.

"The Fixer-Upper's Paradise," he muttered, the name rolling off his tongue like a lumpy dumpling.

He envisioned a haven for the emotionally stunted, the financially challenged, the perpetually confused, and the utterly useless with a screwdriver. And on the other side, a legion of women armed with patience, life coaches, and an inexplicable desire to nurture potential.

Within a week, Felix, with the help of a surprisingly robust online tutorial he'd stumbled upon while trying to find out how to un-flood a kitchen, had cobbled together a rudimentary website.

The aesthetic was deliberately rustic.

Think early 2000. The logo was a cartoon wrench trying to fix a broken heart, both looking equally perplexed.

The categories of "brokenness" was Felix's masterstroke.

Forget "athletic" or "adventurous." Here, you had:

The Emotional Black Hole: Specialises in grunting, avoiding eye contact, and communicating solely through the strategic placement of dirty socks.

The Financial Fiasco: Lives on ramen and dreams of crypto. May or may not have a sofa that doubles as a savings account.

The Domestic Disaster: Believes "clean" is a state of mind, not a physical reality. Has never seen the bottom of his laundry basket.

The Perpetual Peter Pan: Refuses to grow up. Still thinks farts are hilarious. May own a skateboard.

The Existential Enigma: Constantly pondering the meaning of life, usually while forgetting to pay the electricity bill.

The "Everything's Fine" Guy: The most broken of all. Everything is not fine.

Felix launched The Fixer-Upper's Paradise with zero fanfare, mostly because he couldn't figure out how to send out a press release.

He just flicked a switch, then promptly tripped over his cat.

To his astonishment, the website exploded.

Not literally, though given Felix's track record, it was a distinct possibility. Women flocked to it, drawn by the irresistible siren song of a project. Men tired of pretending to be well-adjusted, found solace in openly admitting their flaws.

Take Brenda, a woman who had successfully organised her entire neighbourhood's recycling program and now felt an emptiness only a truly chaotic man could fill.

She found Gary, "The Domestic Disaster," who lived in a perpetual state of controlled chaos. His profile picture was a blurry selfie taken in front of a mountain of unwashed dishes. Brenda saw not a mess, but an opportunity for systematisation. Their first date involved Brenda colour-coding Gary's sock drawer.

It was love at first label.

Or consider Penelope, a therapist who, after a long day of listening to other people's problems, craved a project she could actively take part in.

She matched with Kevin, "The Emotional Black Hole." His profile simply read: "Ugh." Penelope was intrigued. Their first conversation consisted of Penelope asking, "What's 'ugh' about?" and Kevin shrugging for twenty minutes. Penelope called it "progress."

Felix, meanwhile, was overwhelmed.

The server kept crashing.

He'd accidentally signed himself up as "The Everything's Fine Guy," and his inbox was overflowing with messages from women eager to prove him wrong.

He tried to respond to one.

"Hello, I'm Felix, and everything is actually quite not fine; my kitchen is still damp," but his computer froze.

He eventually hired a proper web developer, a stoic woman named Anya, who communicated primarily through code and raised eyebrows. Anya took one look at Felix's original code and let out a sound that, well, sounded like a dying whale.

But she fixed it.

She streamlined the interface, added secure payment options (Felix had forgotten that part), and even designed a "Success Stories" section.

The success stories were truly heartwarming in a bizarre, unconventional way. Gary now had a sparkling kitchen, and a meticulously organised sock drawer thanks to Brenda. Kevin, under Penelope's gentle guidance, had progressed from "Ugh" to "Mildly Annoyed," which, for him, was practically a soliloquy.

Felix, the accidental cupid of chaos, found himself a strange kind of celebrity. He was invited to speak at self-help conventions, though his advice usually devolved into anecdotes about his own ineptitude.

He even started dating, albeit hesitantly.

His own profile; "The Everything's Fine Guy (But Seriously, My Faucet Still Leaks)," attracted a woman named Clara, a retired plumber who found his helplessness endearing. Their first date involved her fixing his faucet while he made her a surprisingly decent cup of tea (he'd finally mastered boiling water).

The Fixer-Upper's Paradise became a phenomenon.

It proved that sometimes, the most perfect match isn't someone who completes you, but someone who's willing to help you put the pieces back together, one slightly bent, water damaged piece at a time.

And Felix, the man who consistently failed upwards, finally understood his true calling: to be the architect of glorious, messy, perfectly imperfect love.

Sign up today!

A REWARD IN THE POETRY SECTION

The musty, comforting scent of old paper and brewing earl grey tea usually permeated "The Bound Page"; a quaint independent bookstore nestled on Argyle Street in the central business district of Northport, New South Wales.

Lately, however, a less charming aroma had wafted through the aisles: the faint, unmistakable tang of mouse.

Not just one mouse, mind you, but an entire extended family of them, who seemed to view the first editions as prime real estate and the poetry section as their personal playground.

Mr Francis Abernathy, the proprietor, a man whose spectacles were perpetually perched on the end of his nose and whose tweed jacket bore the honourable scars of countless literary debates, was at his wit's end.

Traps were set, cheese bait was deployed, and even a stern, whispered lecture about the sanctity of literature was delivered to the skirting boards.

Nothing worked.

The rodents, it seemed, were immune to both conventional pest control and intellectual intimidation.

"What I need," he declared to a dusty copy of Moby Dick, "is a cat. A fierce, predatory beast! A tiny, furry lion of the literary jungle!"

And so, Poe arrived.

Poe was not what one might call "fierce."

She was a sleek, obsidian-furred creature with eyes the colour of ancient amber and a purr that sounded suspiciously like a tiny, contented engine. She was acquired from a local animal shelter, where her file simply stated "Quiet. Enjoys naps. Tolerates petting." Mr Abernathy had envisioned a whiskered warrior, a silent stalker of the stacks. What he got was a connoisseur.

Her first few days were promising.

She stalked.

She pounced.

She batted at dust bunnies with the ferocity of a seasoned hunter.

Mr Abernathy beamed. "That's my girl!" he'd whisper, imagining the terrified squeaks of retreating mice.

Then, the truth slowly emerged.

Poe wasn't stalking mice; she was stalking books.

Specifically, she was stalking the new arrivals table.

She'd rub her head against the spines of freshly unwrapped hardcovers, sniff delicately at the crisp pages, and then, with a sigh of profound satisfaction, settle down for a nap directly on top of the latest Miles Franklin Literary Award prize winner.

The mice, meanwhile, continued their merry little lives, occasionally leaving tiny, incriminating droppings near the philosophy section.

Mr Abernathy's hopes for a rodent-free establishment dwindled, replaced by a growing bewilderment.

Poe was less interested in the food chain and more invested in the literary canon.

Her true calling became apparent one Tuesday afternoon when Ms Higgins, a woman known for her indecisiveness in the fiction aisle, stood pondering between a historical romance and a gritty detective novel.

Poe, who had been meticulously grooming herself atop a display of discounted paperbacks, suddenly sprang into action.

With a determined meow and a surprisingly forceful nudge, Poe head-butted Ms Higgins's ankle, then trotted purposefully towards the "Sydney Morning Herald Bestsellers" display.

She stopped directly in front of a brightly jacketed thriller, looked back at Ms Higgins with an expectant gaze, and then, for good measure, gave the book a gentle, approving tap with her paw.

Ms Higgins, startled but amused, picked up the book. "Well, I never! The cat has an opinion!"

She bought it.

This wasn't a one-off.

It became Poe's modus operandi.

She ignored the scurrying shadows, the gnawed corners of forgotten paperbacks. Her focus was singular: guiding the confused, the browsing, and the utterly lost directly to the literary goldmines.

"Looking for something light?"

Mr Abernathy would hear her purr (or what sounded like a purr of intense literary judgment).

Then, a customer would feel a gentle but firm push against their shin, followed by Poe leading them to the latest feel-good memoir.

"Perhaps a classic?"

A young student overwhelmed by the sheer volume of Shakespeare would find Poe weaving figure-eights around their ankles, ultimately depositing them in front of a beautifully bound copy of Austen's Pride and Prejudice.

Poe would then sit, tail twitching, until the transaction was complete.

Sales of bestsellers skyrocketed.

Customers, initially bewildered by the feline literary critic, found themselves strangely charmed.

"The cat recommended it!" became a common refrain at the checkout counter. Mr Abernathy, despite the ongoing rodent situation (which he now mostly ignored, having accepted his fate), couldn't argue with the improved sales figures. Poe, the bookstore's accidental literary consultant, was a resounding success.

The mice, of course, thrived.

They held tiny, triumphant conventions in the self-help section, occasionally daring to nibble on the corners of Who Moved My Cheese? with a knowing irony.

They knew Poe wasn't their enemy.

She was too busy ensuring humanity was well read.

And as for Poe, she remained blissfully unaware of her original job description, content in her role as the bookstore's most discerning, and furry, literary lioness.

After all, a well-read human was a happy human, and a happy human was more likely to give good head scratches.

And perhaps, just perhaps, leave a stray crumb of croissant near the poetry section.

THE BINDING TRUTH

"You know," Brenda said, leaning against the towering 'New Releases' display, "Mr Finch just bought another five books."

Gary, meticulously alphabetizing the 'True Crime' section for the third time that hour, didn't look up. "Only five? He's slacking. Last Tuesday, it was a baker's dozen of obscure historical biographies and a pop-up book about quantum physics."

Brenda sighed, adjusting her glasses. "I swear, his house must be a fire hazard. Or a very elaborate, literary Jenga tower."

"Or a secret lair," Gary mused, finally turning, a glint in his eye. "Think about it, Brenda. He never actually reads them. Not that we see, anyway. He comes in, browses with an almost reverent intensity, selects his haul, pays in crisp, unmarked bills, always cash, and then vanishes into the literary ether."

"And he always insists on paper bags," Brenda added, tapping her chin. "Even for a single paperback.

"'The plastic crinkles,' he said. 'Disturbs the ambiance,'" she said, mimicking his slightly nasal, overly serious tone.

"Ambiance of what?" Gary chuckled.

"His unread library? His literary fortress of solitude?"

Their unofficial, highly speculative 'Mr Finch Watch' had been a staple of their shifts at 'The Binding Truth' bookstore for months in Northport, New South Wales.

Mr Finch was their enigma, their white whale, their most perplexing regular. He was a man of indeterminate age, always impeccably dressed in tweed, with a perpetually bewildered expression, as if he'd just woken up from an exceptionally long nap in a very dusty attic.

And he bought books. So many books.

"I have a theory," Brenda announced, pushing off the display. "He's building a book fort. Like a literal, structural fort. He's probably got a little reading nook inside, surrounded by thousands of unread tomes, and he just sits there, breathing in the scent of paper and ink, feeling superior."

Gary snorted. "Too simple. My theory is far more complex, and frankly, more thrilling. He's a spy. These aren't books, Brenda. These are cleverly disguised data storage units. Each spine holds a microchip; each page holds a coded message. He buys them, takes them home, extracts the intel, and then, well, I don't know what he does with the empty shells. Maybe he has a giant paper shredder shaped like a literary critic."

"Gary," Brenda said flatly, "he bought 'The Joy of Crocheting' last week. And '101 Delicious Vegan Smoothies'."

"Diversion!" Gary declared, waving a hand dismissively.

"Misdirection! No self-respecting spy would only buy espionage thrillers. That's amateur hour. He's blending in. Who would suspect the man who owns a copy of 'Advanced Macramé Techniques' of being a clandestine operative?"

Brenda had to admit it was more entertaining than the fort theory. "Okay, but what's the intel? Recipes for world domination disguised as smoothie ingredients?"

"Precisely!" Gary snapped his fingers. "Or 'The Joy of Crocheting' is actually a manual for weaving invisible cloaks. Think about it, Brenda. He's never seen reading. He's never seen carrying a book bag. He just appears, buys, and disappears. Invisible cloaks!"

Their theories grew more elaborate with each Mr Finch visit.

He was a dragon, hoarding knowledge like gold, not to use it, but simply to possess it.

He was a sentient algorithm, programmed to gain information but incapable of processing it.

He was an alien trying to understand human culture by accumulating its printed output, but getting hopelessly bogged down in the sheer volume.

One particularly slow Tuesday, Mr Finch came in and bought a first edition of a relatively obscure 19th-century novel, 'The Winding Staircase of Fate', and a children's picture book about a grumpy koala.

"See?" Gary whispered dramatically as Mr. Finch paid.

"The koala book is clearly a coded message for his contact. 'The grumpy koala has landed,' or something equally cryptic."

"Or" Brenda countered, "he just likes koalas. Or he has a grandchild. Or he's trying to learn how to be less grumpy."

Mr Finch paused at the door, clutching his paper bags.

He turned back, his bewildered expression deepening.

"You know," he said, his voice a soft murmur, "I find the mere possession of these narratives immensely comforting. The potential. The promise. It's like having a thousand conversations waiting to happen, without the pressure of actually having them."

He gave a small, almost imperceptible nod, and then, as always, vanished.

Brenda and Gary stared at the empty doorway.

"The potential," Brenda repeated slowly. "The promise."

"He's a philosopher!" Gary exclaimed, his eyes wide.

"He's not reading them because the idea of reading them is more profound than the act itself! He's living in a state of perpetual intellectual foreplay!"

"Or," Brenda said, pulling out her phone, "he's just really into what the Japanese call 'Tsundoku'."

Gary blinked. "Tsun-what now?"

Brenda scrolled. "Tsundoku. It's a Japanese term for the act of buying books and letting them pile up unread. It literally combines 'tsunde-oku' (to pile things up and leave them) and 'dokusho' (to read books)."

Gary's jaw dropped.

"You're telling me there's a word for it? For Mr Finch's entire existence?"

"Apparently," Brenda smirked. "It's a recognised phenomenon. People do it for assorted reasons. Aspirational reading, collecting, comfort in ownership, the idea that they might read them someday."

"So," Gary said slowly, processing this added information, "he's not a spy, not a fort-builder, not a dragon, not an alien, and not a philosopher living in intellectual foreplay."

"Well," Brenda conceded, "he might still be a philosopher, just one with a very specific, culturally recognised habit."

Gary shook his head, a grin spreading across his face.

"Tsundoku. The Unread Library of Mr Finch. It's beautiful. And slightly disappointing. All those hours we spent crafting elaborate narratives of espionage and intergalactic cultural exchange, and he's just a guy who enjoys buying books more than reading them."

"It's still funny," Brenda insisted.

"And now we have a fancy Japanese word for it. We can sound incredibly sophisticated when we discuss his next haul."

"Indeed," Gary said, picking up a copy of 'The Art of Not Giving A F***' and placing it back on the shelf.

"Next time he comes in, I'm going to casually drop 'Tsundoku' into conversation. See if he flinches."

"He won't flinch," Brenda predicted.

"He'll just give you that bewildered look and buy another five books he'll never open. It's his art. His Tsundoku."

And as the afternoon sun faded through the bookstore windows, Brenda and Gary knew their Mr Finch Watch had simply evolved. He was no less of a mystery, just a more accurately labelled one. And the thought of his ever-growing, unread library continued to provide endless, humorous fodder for their shifts. The Binding Truth, indeed.

ABOUT THE AUTHOR

José F. Nodar is an Australian-Cuban author, reviewer, and literary entrepreneur based in Spring Farm, NSW. He is the founder of Quick Story Tales Online and World Book Reviews, initiatives supporting and promoting both emerging and established authors worldwide.

José's writing blends humour, sentiment, and quiet realism, often drawing from the landscapes and community spirit of regional New South Wales. His fiction, including Whispers from My Wife, The Northport Coffee Group, and Stories to Share with My Partner Collection, explores universal themes of love, loss, and rediscovery.

When not writing, José can be found reading at a local café, walking along Spring Farm's footpaths, or championing local authors and creative groups through interviews and newsletters.

Please visit https://worldbookreviews.com.au/ and let me know what you thought of this book of short stories and poetry.

Good, bad, or indifferent, I will always welcome your hon-est opinion.

Send me an email at info@jfnodar.com.au

Thank you for your purchase!

OTHER BOOKS BY JOSÉ F. NODAR

Novels in English
- The Danny Monk Trilogy
- Books, Pens & Larceny
- Mending Hearts at Crystal Cove
- A Love Finally Spoken
- The Mallard E. Benson Trilogy
- The Girl Who Didn't Come Home
- The Ones That Got Away
- The Ghost We Owe

Mystery
- The Ghost Detective's First Case
- The Northport Coffee Group

Romance

- The Teacher's Assistant
- A Night of Love
- Maybe This Is Everything
- Love in Stereo
- When Love Remembers

Science Fiction & Fantasy

- The Compass Legacy
- The Universe Between Us
- The Time Bus
- The Last Light of Aurethis

Children

The Hamster Who Whispered Back

Humour

- SEX

Collections of Stories and Poetry

- Stories to Share with My Partner Book 1
- Stories to Share with My Partner Book 2
- Stories to Share with My Partner Book 3
- Stories to Share with My Partner Book 4
- Stories to Share with My Partner Book 5
- Stories to Share with My Partner Book 6
- Stories to Share with My Partner Book 7
- Stories to Share with My Partner Book 8
- Stories to Share with My Partner Book 9
- Stories to Share with My Partner Book 10
- Stories to Share with My Partner Book 11
- Stories to Share with My Partner Book 12

Anthologies of Stories and Poetry

- Quick Stories & Poems Volume I
- Quick Stories & Poems Volume 2
- Quick Stories & Poems Volume 3

Libros en Español

La Trilogía de Danny Monk

- Un Amor Expresado

- Reparando Corazones en Crystal Cove

- Un Amor Finalmente Declarado

Colecciones de Cuentos y Poemas

- Cuentos Para Compartir con Mi Pareja Libro 1

- Cuentos Para Compartir con Mi Pareja Libro 2

- Cuentos Para Compartir con Mi Pareja Libro 3

Ciencia Ficción y Fantasía

- El Autobús del Tiempo